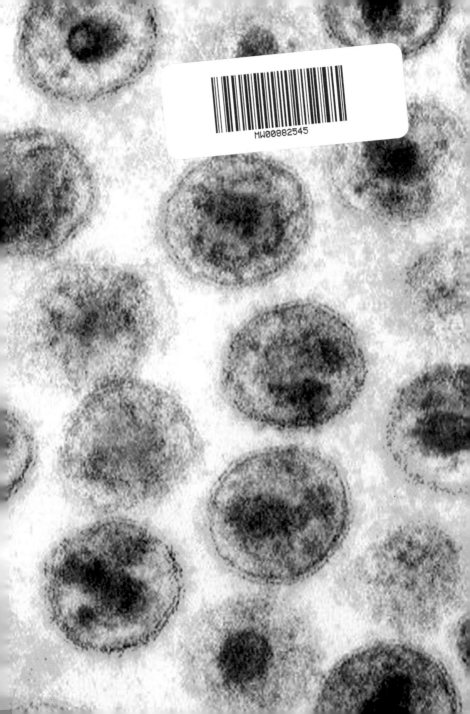

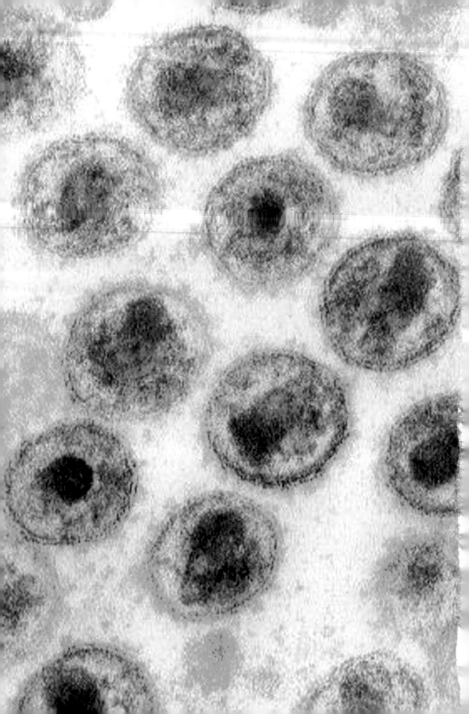

BLOOD BROTHERS

by Rob Sanders

Reycraft Books
55 Fifth Avenue
New York, NY 10003

Reycraftbooks.com

Reycraft Books is a trade imprint and trademark of Newmark Learning, LLC.

Text © 2022 Rob Sanders

Educators and Librarians: Our books may be purchased in bulk for promotional, educational,or business use. Please contact sales@reycraftbooks.com.

Library of Congress Control Number: 2022901716

Hardcover ISBN: 978-1-4788-6927-6
Paperback ISBN: 978-1-4788-6928-3

Photo Credits: Jacket Front A, Front Cover A, Jacket Back, Back Cover: Andrea_Hill/Getty Images; Jacket Front B, Front Cover B: RobinOlimb/Getty Images; Jacket Front C, Front Cover C: filo/Getty Images; Jacket Spine, Book Spine: ARTIKAL/Shutterstock; Front End Paper ii-iv, Rear End Paper i-iii: Callista Images/Getty Images; Page iv: Mike Kuhlman/Shutterstock; Interior backgrounds: studio2013/Shutterstock; Page 460,462: millicookbook/Shutterstock

Author photo: Courtesy of Rob Sanders, photo by Candy Barnhisel

Printed in Dongguan, China. 8557/0822/19451
10 9 8 7 6 5 4 3 2

First Edition Hardcover published by Reycraft Books 2022.

Reycraft Books and Newmark Learning, LLC, support diversity and the First Amendment, and celebrate the right to read.

To RP:
You said we would celebrate the person I am.
Thank you for helping me do just that.

In memory of TM and RM—
my first friends lost to AIDS.

Though inspired by actual events,
this book is a work of fiction.

DAY 1
SATURDAY
AUGUST 15, 1987

1

Charlie is the best at dying.

I watch him across the beach.
He scans the clouds.
Presses his stick rifle against one shoulder.
Aims out over the waves.
The wind licks at his sun-bleached hair,
ruffling tufts of it over
his squinted eyes.

I dig good trenches.

Three of them line up side-by-side,
fortified with driftwood
anchored deep in the
oatmeal-colored sand.

Swaying salt grass hides the
trenches from our
invisible enemy.

The beach.
Our beach.
The perfect place to battle.
The perfect place to fight.

The safest perfect place we know.

Attackers! Curtis calls. *High noon!*

Man your stations, I order.
I push my body against the grit.
Eyes dart across the horizon.
From cloud to cloud.
East to west.
I spot them.
Wait for it . . . wait for it . . . NOW!

Rat-a-tat-tat.
Th-th-th-th-th-th-th.
Kapow. Kapow. Kapow.

Driftwood weapons fire.

Charlie's elbows rest
on the rim of one trench.
He fires again and again and again.

Kapow. Bang-bang. Kapow.

Curtis crouches nearby,
curls of brown hair
stuck to his forehead
His body recoiling
with each
stick-rifle
blast.

Incoming! Charlie hollers.
I scramble into the trench
with my brothers.
We hunker down,
like in the tornado drills
back at Ashland Elementary.

We take a blow.
Handfuls of sand rain down.

Rat-a-tat-tat.
   Kapow. Kapow. Kapow.
      Th-th-th-th-th-th-th.

I'm hit, Charlie groans.
He waves his arms, spins,
falls face-first into the sand,
flops his legs, sputters, spits.
Takes one last breath.

Always the best at dying.

> *Damn them!* Curtis screams—
> breaking one of Momma's rules.

He aims,
slowly moving the barrel of
his weapon, tracing the path
of the enemy planes.
The ones only
he can see.
He fires.
Curses at the clouds.

Ka-plew. Ka-plew. Ka-plew.

Charlie may die good,
but Curtis wins for sound effects.
Take that, he hollers.

My shoulder, I yell,
dropping my weapon.
Both hands clutch
my wound and I fall back,
                    back,
            back
into the sandy pit.

Curtis jerks, gasps.

They got me, too.
He tumbles in beside me.

One sweaty dead brother
on the right.
Another on the left.

Anger rises from my belly,
higher and higher
until it pushes
out through
my lips.
My brothers, I scream.
Not my brothers!

I claw up
out of the pit.
Try to stand.
Sway.
Gain my balance.
Aim.
Pull the trigger . . .

                     nothing.

Pull it again . . .

                     nothing.

I'm out of am . . .

Rat-a-tat-tat. Rat-a-tat-tat.

The word *ammo*
sticks in my throat.
It's my turn to moan.
Grabbing my gut, I collapse
back into the trench on top
of Curtis and Charlie.
My legs too long
to fit inside.

We lay still.
Quiet.
Waves, sea gulls,
and our heavy breathing—
the only sounds we hear.

> *Let's play again,* Charlie says
> from under the pile.
> > *Only if we don't have to die again,*
> > Curtis replies.

Ain't gonna happen, I say.
That's the way we play this game.
No changes allowed.

It always ends like this—
panting,
sweating,
hearts pounding.
And then we're dead.

The Johnston brothers—
side by side,
motionless,
bodies in the ground.

My sweat-soaked T-shirt
feels like a weight, pushing
me deep into the sand.
Sweat rolls off my forehead,
streaks down my cheeks,
runs through the creases of my neck.

Change the game? Nope.
I'm keeping things—anything,
everything—the same.
Keeping things—anything,
everything—from changing more than they already have.
Even a stupid game of war at the beach.
No changes allowed.

Lying in a pit with my brothers . . . again.
Playing dead . . . again.
I'm okay with that.
Okay with keeping
things exactly
the same.

2

Damn fine dying, fellas.

It's Izzy.
I know it without looking up
or climbing out of the trench.
There's no mistaking that girl's gruff voice.

Izzy's my best friend.
Has been since I don't know when.
Even if she is a girl.
Even if she does live
at the beach,
which makes me as
jealous as all get out.
Even if we do live
sixty-five miles apart
and only see each
other when Momma
decides to haul us
to the cabin.

I look up to say hello.
And.
Stop.

She's like a shampoo commercial
coming toward me.
Wearing a red bikini.
  Where're the cut-offs and T-shirt?
Blonde hair blowing around her face.
  What happened to the Yankees cap?

  When did she grow those?
Charlie asks.
   Hush, Curtis shushes.

Honestly,
I was wondering
the same thing.

How long has it been
since we were at the beach?
A month? Two?
Obviously, long enough.

I climb out of the pit.
Run a sand-covered hand
through my sweaty hair.
Throw my shoulders back.
Try to look as grown up as Izzy.
Like I could compete with her.
With those.

Hell, Poet Boy. Cat got your tongue?

Charlie clicks his,
like Momma would.

Momma loves Izzy,
but she can't stand cussing.

Izzy can't seem to stop.
Momma says she cusses like a sailor.
Truth is, Izzy cusses like a grandfather—
the one she lives with.

If she lived with us,
Izzy'd be filling up
Momma's Cuss Jar—
one quarter at a time.

      You found any turtle nests yet?
      Curtis asks.

Two, Izzy answers.
Down near our place.
Got 'em roped off . . .
from tourists.

She rolls her eyes
at the thought of tourists.
Lowest number of nests ever.
Damndest thing I've ever seen.

The way Izzy cusses,
Momma could collect enough quarters
to put us all through college.
Of course, that'll never happen
if they don't let us back
into school.

Most kids wouldn't complain about
not going to school.
But when someone says
you can't do something,
you want to do it,
no matter what.
And when something
isn't fair, it makes you—
it makes me—
want to
fill up the
Cuss Jar
all
by
myself.

3

**If Izzy thinks homeschooling is weird,
she's never said anything.**

If she knew why
we do school at home,
she might have
lots to say.
But that's a secret.

Izzy thinks I can't keep a secret.
Especially from her.
I've tried
keeping
secrets.
I kept my poetry
a secret for a
long time.
I thought poetry
would seem
dumb to Izzy.
Then Momma told her.
Poetry wasn't
dumb
after
all.

When it comes
to me keeping secrets,
Izzy's wrong.
Dead wrong.

I've gotten good at
not telling stuff.
Or just telling the part
of something I
want someone
to know.

Homeschool's one
of those half secrets.
Izzy thinks it was
Momma's idea.
Momma would
get a good laugh
out of that one.
Izzy has no
idea we were
kicked out of
school . . . or why.
Why is the
biggest
secret
of all.

Even if she doesn't
know, it makes

me feel good
that Izzy doesn't act like
going to school
at home
is weird.
She doesn't even
act like me writing
poems is weird.
Not that she's ever
seen my poems
or read 'em.
If she had an opinion,
she'd tell me.
Izzy doesn't
keep opinions
to herself.

When it comes to school, Izzy's never liked it anyway.
    The beach is my classroom, she said once,
        sounding like the narrator on a nature
        documentary.

*Why don't you say,
Screw school, I wanna
be outside?* I asked
in my best TV
reporter voice.

Screw school,
I wanna be outside,
she replied.

Even though Izzy
doesn't like school,
she's smart.
Real smart.
She knows a lot of things
about a lot of things.

> How to spot dolphins in calm water.
> > How long it takes sea turtles to hatch.
> > > Which plants are native to
> > > Florida and which aren't.
> How to shuffle your feet to scare off
> stingrays.
> > The secret to gutting a fish and
> > frying it up on a campfire.
> > > Where manatees go to find
> > > warm water.

I guess me not going to school
isn't a big deal to Izzy.
But to me,
It's a big deal.
A
   really
big deal.

I miss the smell of the library.
Miss research projects.
Miss doing book reports.
Even miss spelling tests.

We do all those things
in home school.
But
it's
not
the
same.
Home is home.
School is school.
And if school is at home,
then something
is missing.
Something
has changed.

There's that word again.
Change.

Izabelle Lawrence, did I hear what I think I heard?

Momma seems to
appear out of nowhere,
stepping out from behind
a sea-oats-covered dune.
She catches Izzy red-handed—
        or red-tongued—
                or whatever you'd call catching
                someone cussing.

        Sorry, Momma J., Izzy says.
        She runs over for a hug.
        Momma acts like she's
        completely forgotten
        the four-letter word already.

If it had been me,
        or Curtis,
                or Charlie
                (like Charlie would ever cuss),
we'd never hear
the end of it.
        Even after the quarters clunked into the jar.

Look at you, girl, Momma begins,
noticing what we all noticed
a few minutes before.
You're turning into a beauty.
A pretty young woman like you
shouldn't use dirty language like that.

    Yes, ma'am.
    Izzy looks all sorry like.

Of course, I know
she'll be cussing again,
as soon as Momma's out of sight.

Cussing's not the only thing
Momma doesn't like.
She doesn't like war
    or guns—
      even if it's pretend.
She can't stand the sight of blood.
And she doesn't like boys getting sweaty and smelly.

I hope someone's
gonna fill in those holes,
Momma says,
pointing to the trenches.
A person could stumble
in and break a leg.

We'll fill 'em in, I say,
when we're
finished
playing.

Bad choice of words.

Playing? You call war "play"?
You boys have a lot to learn.
Don't they, Izzy?
Of course, Izzy agrees,
shaking her head like
she can hardly believe
how stupid we are.

And you boys make sure
to wash off all that sand
before coming up to the cabin.
How could a woman who
loves the beach so much,
dislike sand so much?

Three other things top
Momma's don't-like list—
lies,
selfish people,
and funerals.
She can't stand talking about
dying,

or graves,
or obituaries,
or anything else on the subject of dying.

I suppose dying
is on my
don't-like list, too.
But sometimes
living isn't
all that great
either.
And it sure isn't
easy.
Not now
anyway.

As for dying, no one likes that,
or talking about it.
But everyone does it.
Die, I mean.

5

Yep, those kids are mine,

Momma says to some
stranger she's met on the beach.
A Sandy Beach tourist, I guess,
since she's paler than clouds.

Curtis and Charlie
are jumping waves.
I'm sitting by Izzy.
She's laid out on a towel,
sunglasses on,
bikini brighter
than the sun.
I scratch at the sand with a stick.

Momma thinks no one's listening.
I am.

The little one's Charlie—my baby—he's my love bug.
Curtis—he's the middle one—all boy,
and the man of the family.
The one sitting over there,

that's Calvin—he's my oldest—
a thinker, not a doer.
Just like his daddy.
Loves to read and write.

A thinker, not a doer.
Just like my daddy.
Was it supposed to be a compliment?
It doesn't feel like one.
A thinker seems like nothing
compared to being the man of the family.
That should be *my* job.
I thought it was my job.
And what good does thinking do?
I don't think
a thinker
is much to be.
A doer.
Now that's something.
And I wanna be something.
A thinker?
No thanks.
Like my daddy?
No thanks to that, too.
Like I said,
I wanna *be* something.

Momma's conversation pauses.

The tourist says something.
Momma looks back in our direction,
then says,

Oh, her? That's Izzy.
She's my beach daughter.
She and Calvin grew up teething on seashells,
and eating fistfuls of sand.
She's always been one of the boys.
But by the looks of things, that's changing fast.

When we were little,
Momma and the three of us boys
practically lived at the beach.
Izzy and I did everything together.
She *was* like one of the boys.
One of the family.

When school started for me,
        then Curtis,
                and finally Charlie—
summers and weekends
became our beach time.
That's when Izzy and I
started our twice-a-week phone calls.

Then we got the diagnosis—
        Izzy doesn't know even one part of that secret—

and Momma lost her job,
and the car got kind of iffy,
and getting to the beach got harder,
and Izzy and I got even better with phone calls.
Sitting in our kitchens 65 miles apart,
talking, or not talking,
till someone made us hang up.

You're the jelly to my peanut butter,
I told her on one of those calls.
I'd heard some kids at the Pick-and-Pay say it.
As soon as the words came out of my mouth,
I knew they were dumb.

> *How stupid,* Izzy said,
> breaking into a laugh.

But that's how close we are,
I tried to explain,
mad and embarrassed,
but laughing, too.

> *Come on, Poet Boy,*
> *you can do better than that.*
> *How about . . .*
> > *. . . the pearl to my oyster?*
> > *. . . or the snorkels to my flippers?*
> > *. . . or the fly to my rod?*

I got real quiet

You there?

Izzy, I finally said.

Yes?

I let the silence go on a bit longer,
then in my best Hollywood actor voice:
You're the fish eyes to my fish guts.

That got a roaring laugh
and started a 30-minute long analogy-a-thon.
A warm feeling crawled from my toes
to the top of my head
as we found as many
gross ways to say we're
friends—best friends—
without really saying it.

We're connected—Izzy and me.
        Fish eyes
        and
        fish guts.
That's never gonna change.

Momma talks to the woman
the rest of the afternoon.
But I know she doesn't tell the tourist everything.

Momma definitely doesn't tell the one secret
about her boys that would send
the woman running back home
as quick as her pale
white legs would
take her.

6

There's bad blood in our family.

It's something we've all got.
Three brothers. Three bleeders.
We've known it for a long time.

Hemophiliacs doctors call it.
Our blood doesn't clot right.
The littlest thing—a cut,
        a fall from a bike,
                pulling a tooth,
                        taking a bad bounce
                              from a baseball

and we bleed—a lot.

Can't come to the beach,
can't be in the cabin,
without knowing,
remembering,
thinking
a little of that
bad blood
has flowed
through
our family
for years.
That's how
you get it.
Through
family.
From Dutch
to Momma.
From Momma
to us.

We gotta have blood.
So they give us stuff
to make our blood clot—
stuff made from other people's blood.

It's easy.

A needle in your arm.

It hurts, but you get used to it.

A clear bag of stuff hanging above your head.

A plastic tube running from the bag to the needle.

Gravity pulling the stuff down through the tube,

      into your arm,

            into your blood,

                  pumping through your heart,

                        moving to every part of

                            your body.

D
  r
    i
      p.
D
  r
    i
      p.
D
  r
    i
      p.

Little drops. Powerful things.

The doctors didn't know . . .

and the nurses didn't know . . .

and my Momma didn't know . . .

and my brothers didn't know . . .
and I sure didn't know that

d
  r
    o
      p

by

d
  r
    o
      p

by

d
  r
    o
      p

the blood we needed to live
could end up killing us.

7

Folks say Momma should have kept her mouth shut,

because if she never wrote that letter,
then the School Board would've never known.

And if the School Board didn't know,
then they never would've written back.

> *We regret to inform you . . .*
> *Due to the illness . . .*
> *For the safety and well-being of others. . .*
> *Your boys cannot attend school.*

Momma said not telling
wasn't an option.
It's the right thing to do.

She thought if she did the right thing,
everyone else would, too.
Sometimes the right thing
        can end up
                going all wrong.
And it did.

The Ashland City School District kicked us out.

Ashland schools are stupid anyway.
They don't even have a middle school.
Make sixth graders stay with elementary kids
until they're in seventh grade and go to the junior high.
Who needs that?
Who needs them?

But even though it's a stupid school
in a stupid town,
sometimes I kind of wish
Momma would've kept her mouth shut.

AIDS [eydz]
Acquired Immune Deficiency Syndrome
noun, *Pathology*

> a disease of the immune system characterized
> by increased susceptibility to opportunistic
> infections, as pneumocystis carinii pneumonia
> and candidiasis, to certain cancers, as Kaposi's
> sarcoma, and to neurological disorders: caused
> by a retrovirus and transmitted chiefly through
> blood or blood products that enter the body's
> bloodstream, especially by sexual contact or
> contaminated hypodermic needles. The disease
> may also be passed from mother to child in
> childbirth, and through blood transfusions. AIDS
> results from Human Immunodeficiency Virus (HIV).

A nurse gave us a brochure
with the definition.
One sheet of paper,
front and back,
folded in thirds.

That's all we had.

That's all we knew.
At first.
That was enough.
At first.

The doctor told
Momma and me
while Curtis and Charlie
sat in the waiting room.
Momma wanted to leave me there, too.
I wouldn't let her.
I almost wish I had.

The doctor told us
the diagnosis,
about protocols,
and what
they were
going to do
about
the HIV.

He said,
>   *Do this.*
>   *Don't do that.*
>   *Come back in a month.*
>   *Watch for signs of illness.*
>   *Call if there are any questions or problems.*

Questions?
I was full of them.
But I didn't ask any.

He told us about
experimental drugs.
New treatments.
About AZT.
And that it's not
approved
for kids . . .
yet.

They'll treat the symptoms.
Keep us strong.

There could be a new med
any day.
Might be a cure
within a year.

I knew, when
there's a *could*,
there could be a *could not*.
And when there's a *might*,
there might be a *might not*.

Three brothers,
with tanned skin
and hair that
flaps in the
gulf breeze.

One diagnosis.

Three brothers,
who play war
at the beach.

One disease.

Charlie knows we're sick.
  That we have to stay healthy.
Curtis and I know more.
  That it's hard for kids to get HIV or AIDS.
  That it was in the blood. The transfusions.
  That we can expose others to the virus.

I wanted—needed—to know more.
I tried looking it up.
It's so new it's not in the
dictionary or encyclopedia.
There are no books about it
in the Ashland City Library either.

Then I found the news magazines in the stacks in the
back of the library.
In a cold room behind two metal doors
with fluorescent lights that seemed to
quiver as they glowed.
Found more than I wanted to know.
Found more than I needed to know.
Found more than I could
write in a poem.
Even if I wrote
poems until the
day I die.

9

Who's coughing? Momma calls from the back of the cabin.

Charlie! Curtis and I yell back.
Traitors, Charlie says.

None of us want to be caught
coughing,
or sneezing,
or breathing funny
around Momma.
One little thing
and here comes
the thermometer
and Tylenol.

Come here, Momma says,
walking into the living room.
Let's take your temperature.

Momma, Charlie moans.

Don't Momma me.
We're not having you getting sick.
Not at the beach.
Not before it's time
to go back to school.
Not . . . not ever.

She's the momma bird making sure all her young are
safe in the nest.
Flaps her wings and hops into action at the first sign of
anyone being sick.
A little cough—
         could turn into pneumonia.
A sneeze or breathing funny—
         could be respiratory problems.
We're not normal kids any more.
We're kids with HIV.

Hold it under your tongue and hush.
Charlie lets Momma Bird do her thing.

Momma's gonna treat the symptoms—
         every one of them—
                  like the doctor said.
It's all she can do.

Momma doesn't
have control
of everything
that happens to

her babies.
Not anymore.
So whatever
she has control
over—she does.
And she does it
a lot.

I don't like her hovering.
Waiting for a sniffle, or itch, or earache.
I hide my symptoms from her.
Treat them myself.
Momma doesn't need to know everything.
Doesn't need to worry any more than she already does.

She's scared.
I think.
Any mom would be.
I guess.
Momma birds are supposed to be able to take care of
their babies.
Baby birds are supposed to be able to grow up and
leave the nest.
Things don't always work out the way they're supposed
to.

I bet Momma gets tired
of not being able
to take care of
everything herself.

I bet she doesn't
want anything else
to change either.

I'm a lot like Momma Bird.

Facts. Statistics. Data. Charts.

That's what was in the magazines
in the stacks
in the cold room
behind the metal doors
in the Ashland City Library.

Data and charts.
Facts and statistics.
>AZT only takes away symptoms.
>HIV *will* become AIDS.
>There's no known cure.
>No one survives.

But the magazines had more than facts and statistics.
They had photographs.
>Some of doctors.
>Some of labs making medicines.
>Some of guys with sores on their bodies.
>Some of young men sick in bed.
>Some of them dying in bed.

Alone in the hospital.
Skin and bones.
Gasping for breath.
Eyes frozen in time.
Wanting to live.
Waiting to die.

I reached under my T-shirt.
Ran a hand over my stomach,
up to my chest,
over my shoulders.
When would I look like them?
When would I be covered with sores,
gasping for breath?

I wanted to close the magazines.
I wanted to walk away.
I wanted to leave everything in the
stacks of the Ashland City Library.
I wanted to let the metal doors slam
on the cold-as-a-morgue room with
        its flickering lights
                and the pictures that seemed to be
                        fortune-tellers predicting
                        my future.

But I kept looking.
Kept turning the pages.
Kept touching the photos.

That's AIDS.
Right there.
Printed on paper.
More real than facts and statistics.
More real than a brochure folded in thirds.
That was all I needed—wanted—to know.

I didn't tell anyone.
I didn't show anyone.
I carried the pictures around in my brain.

I still dream about those photos.
And my dream
> always
> ends
> with
> three
> empty
> beds
> side
> by
> side.

11

That's the biggest secret I've kept from Izzy.

She knows about the bleeding.
She doesn't know about the HIV.
She knows about us being homeschooled.
She doesn't know we've been kicked out of practically
everything in Ashland, or why.

No reason to tell her.
Wouldn't do any good.
Would only worry her.
We're not going to give it to her,
so what's it matter?

Telling her wouldn't
change anything.
I think.
But I don't want
to find out.

It does seem kinda weird though,
since Izzy's the
only person
I ever
really

talk
to.

The kind of talking
that you can't
do with your
brothers or
your mother
because
the thoughts
are mixed
up with
feelings,
and they're
not just
about
your own
little
life,
but
bigger.
Bigger thoughts.
Bigger ideas.
About the world.
About the universe.

We've been that way
since we were little.
We'll be playing tackle tag one minute,
and sitting cross-legged

talking about a book we read,
or what Dan Rather said on
the CBS Evening News
the next.

We talk about the kind
of stuff normal kids do,
and other stuff they'd
think is stupid.

Books.
Sports.
War.
Politics.
Unfair things.
Hunger.
Who died.
Who lied.
Who tried
to save
the world.

Deeper than deep,
that's what
Izzy calls it.

The two of us want to:
Change the world.
Be remembered.
Do something.

Something
important.

What kid thinks about that?
Us.

And Izzy's the only person
I've ever
really
listened
to.

The kind
of listening
that makes
you squint
your eyes,
trying to
understand.

The kind
of listening
where you
try not to
interrupt.

Not thinking
your own
thoughts.
Not getting

ready to say
something
as soon
as the
other
person
takes
a breath.

Listening.
Squinting.
Nodding.

Izzy listens, too.

I'm sure she would listen to the
worst secret in the world.
The secret that's not a secret
to almost anyone any more.

Except
          my
                    best
                              friend.

But I don't want
my best friend
to know
my worst secret.

12

Have you heard about this AIDS thing? Izzy asks.

It's our last chance to hang out before I head back
to Ashland.
We sit around what's left of a fire.
Wrapped in towels
against the breeze.
Damp bathing
suits soaking
through.

We've already discussed
President Reagan's speech at the Berlin Wall,
the new Canadian Loonie coin,
The Whipping Boy,
and Don Mattingly's homerun streak,
so no topic should surprise me.
This one does.

> *No*, I lie.

Really? It's in the news all the time.

I'm silent.
Looking down at the sand.
Hoping its dark enough to
hide the clammy
fear that feels
like it's crawling
up my body
and snatching
away my breath.

Even the president's talking about it.
Finally, she adds.
Like that will help me remember.
Or understand.

Still silent.
Picking at my sandals.
Thoughts tripping over each other in my brain.
Not now.
Let's not talk about this now.
Let's keep things like they are.
Not now.

It's this disease that's been spreading for a few years.
Mostly in big cities—New York, San Francisco,
even Miami.
Liberace died from it.

Who?
My fingers dig deep

into the sand
on both sides
of me.

Liberace—that old piano player.

    So?

So, it's an epidemic. No cure.

    Okay. So?

*It's a horrible disease. But I guess we don't need to
worry about it.*

    I look up at her for the first time.
    Waiting for her to say more.
    My hands have dug a trench
    that goes almost all the way around me.
    A moat—maybe—to keep Izzy out.
    A wall—maybe—to keep my secret in.
    Something to keep her from seeing
    the feelings that are about to come
    rolling out of my eyes at any minute now.

Only gay guys get it.

    What?

Homos. Queers. They're the only ones who get AIDS.

That's a lie.

The words spit out
before I can stop them.

What?

My face burns as red
as the coals in the fire.
I can feel it from the inside.
My heart beats anger through my body.
My breath's raggedy. I gasp for air,
like I've been underwater too long.
And I'm shivering.
Or shaking.
Or both.

That's a frigging lie!

Whataya mean? She cocks her head to one side.
You said you didn't know anything about it.

I jump up.
Sand falls off me
like dead skin.
I walk away.
Feet sinking in the sand
with each step.

Calvin? What's wrong?
What did I say?
Where are you going?

My walk turns into a trot.
Then a full-out sprint.
My feet beat into the beach,
sand slinging up behind.

That's a lie, Izzy!
I scream.

My voice is carried away by the wind.
Drowned out by the surf.
I gasp for breath
like a man
sinking
below
the
surface
of a
giant
pool of
quicksand.

Calvin!
her voice calls after me.

DAY 2
SUNDAY
AUGUST 16, 1987

1

I bet everyone in Ashland is hacked off.
I bet their blood is boiling.

Sunday papers are plopping on front porches,
and probably in some bushes, too.
There it is in black and white.
Judge's decision on the
front page—

> *No reason*
> *medically or legally*
> *to keep the Johnston brothers*
> *out of school.*

No reason except
no one wants
us near
their
kids.

Kids we've known since kindergarten.
Kids from our scout troop.
Kids from our little league teams.
Kids from our church camp.

Curtis takes one look at the paper and says,
We should celebrate!
I don't think he's serious,
but just in case I reply,

    Let's not.

        We could have cake, and balloons, and
        fireworks.
        I know Charlie's not joking.

          Cake we could do, Momma says.
          But I think our celebration
          needs to be on the quiet side.

    There'll be enough fireworks
    going off in Ashland, I say,
    when folks see the paper.

We got something we deserved.
Going to school's something every kid's supposed to do.
It shouldn't be something you need to celebrate.
It's something to be expected.
Momma had to fight for it.
That wasn't right.
And we won.

Which is what we wanted.
But a party?
A celebration?
No thanks.

Well, I'm glad it's over, Curtis says.

                    Almost did me in, Momma replies.
        She smiles, but I can tell . . .
                . . . she's serious.

        It's not over, I say.
        Not 'til we're sitting at desks
        in Ashland Elementary School.
        Besides, these people aren't gonna give up
        all that easy. They're . . .

                Hacked off? Charlie asks.

                Momma nods. *Yep.*

Truth is, these people—
        the kids in the scout troop,
        and the little league,
        and church camp,
        and their parents—
                        hack me off.
                        Big time.

Must be admitted—
So ordered . . .

2

Below the headline,

and before the article
in small black type—
Ashland, Florida (AP)

Associated Press.
Our story isn't an Ashland story anymore.

Lots of newspapers print AP stories.
I know that from writing research papers.
This article could be in
papers all over Florida . . .
all across the country . . .
all around the world.

I breathe in a chest full of pride.
People around the world may know my name.
    And Curtis'.
        And Charlie's.
            They may know we were
            kicked out of school.
                They may know our
                Momma fought to
                get us back in.

They may know we stood up to all of Ashland.
    At least Momma and the lawyer did.
        Everyone in the world may
        know we're the brothers
        with HIV.

The air in my lungs begins
to turn into carbon dioxide.
    The brothers with HIV—
        everyone in the world knows—
            we're the brothers with HIV.

My chest full of pride turns to a
    chest full of fear,
        or embarrassment,
            or poison.

I exhale the air
    and the feelings
        from my lungs.
        Out of my mouth.
        Quick as I can.
Trying to get rid of it.
Trying to not feel like the whole world
just saw me naked.
In fact, naked might not be as bad as this.

Izzy, I whisper.

I imagine Gramps Lawrence heading to In-a-Sack

to grab his morning coffee.
A cruller.
A Sunday newspaper.
I can see him finding the article.
Heading home.
Shoving the paper at Izzy.
My secret.
My secret could be in Izzy's hands right now.
She could be reading every detail at this second.

She's gonna hate me.
It's the first thought in my brain
and it comes out of my mouth
with a puff of air.
I'm a liar.
That's my second thought.
Izzy would say not saying anything is the same as lying.
And it is.
Not saying anything is not telling the truth.
It's a lie.

I have a disease that could—

                that will—

                                kill me.

For over a year,
I've kept the biggest secret ever
from my best friend.

I can see her wadding up the paper.
Throwing it in the trash.
Throwing away our friendship.
All because
          I'm a liar.

She's going to hate me, I whisper again.
I bet she already does.

Because words have a way of spreading,

the second letter we got last year
was from Reverend Otis Walker of the
Open Door Fellowship Church.

A hand-delivered-we-regret letter—
               like the one from school—
                             only totally different.

No, thank you, Rev. Walker said
when Momma invited him in.
        The boys would love to visit with you,
        Pastor, Momma said.
It wasn't true.
At least not for me.
Having a preacher in my house,
well, that's not what I call an enjoyable afternoon.

No, Rev. Walker replied.
It was almost a screech.
                    A yelp.
                        A scared sound.
No need to bother the boys.
I wanted to drop this off, Carolyn.

His voice back to normal.
Handed Momma an envelope.
I met with the deacons last night.
They . . . we . . . decided . . . you know . . .
about all that's going on right now.
It's all in the letter.
God bless you, Carolyn,
and your boys.
Just like that,
he turned.
Walked
away.

Momma tore into the envelope.
Read it.
Still standing in the doorway.
        If that doesn't beat all.
Shook her head.
        And God bless you, Reverend,
she mumbled, closing the door.

I found the letter that afternoon,
on the kitchen table.
It was all about love,
and being there for us.
As long as *there*
wasn't
anywhere
near
them.

We're like the lepers
in that Bible story.
Unclean.
Untouchable.
Unwanted.

Who knew you could get kicked out of church?
Wish I'd known that sooner.

I could've slept in all those Sundays.

4

The church bell clangs twice.
9:30.
Sunday school's starting.

I don't miss church.
Not one bit.
Curtis and Charlie do.

Curtis misses charming
the old women into
giving him hugs,
and chewing gum,
and butterscotch candies
right out of their purses.

Charlie misses singing,
raising his hands in praise,
listening to the organ squawk,
shouting *Amen* along
with all the deacons of
Open Door Fellowship.

When he hears the church bell,
Charlie launches into a song,
right there in the middle of the living room,

standing on the sofa,
waving his hands
through the air.

There's power, power,
      wonder-working power.
            In the precious blood of the Lamb.

We've got power in our blood, too.
Enough to scare everyone in town.

Before I know it,
Charlie starts up his second hymn.

There is sunshine in my soul today,
            More glorious and bright . . .

Twelve orbits around the sun.
That's all it's taken to get me here.

Ten orbits for Curtis.
Nearly eight for Charlie.

The Johnston boys,
racing around the sun.
Trying for as many orbits
as we can get.
Hoping for them.
Wishing for them.

O there's sunshine, blessed sunshine,
*   While the peaceful, happy moments roll;*
When Jesus shows His smiling face
*   There is sunshine in my soul.*

5

**What's this word, Charlie asks, *looking up
from the newspaper.***

     Infected, I answer.

Infected Boys Must Be . . .
He pauses.
Looks at me.
Waits for help.

     Allowed.

Infected Boys Must Be Allowed In.

That's the front page headline.
Charlie stares at the page.
Are we the boys?

     Yep.

What's infected mean?

     Sick, I reply.
     Short and simple.

Oh, he nods. *The HIV.*

I nod, too.

On page two,
another headline:

School Board Meeting—Monday
Topic: Student Health and Safety
Special guest: CDC Representative

CDC = Centers for Disease Control
3 boys + Bad blood = Disease

Paper says the person's
coming down from Atlanta
to speak on the Johnstons' behalf.

> *Momma*, I call.
> *Do we know this CDC man?*
> *And why he's coming from Atlanta?*

> *No. And no*, she hollers from the kitchen.

Coming on our behalf.
I didn't invite him.
Momma didn't invite him.
Our lawyer didn't invite him.

You can be (insert cuss word here)
sure the School Board didn't invite him.

Ashland's dead on the Lord's Day.

Especially after church lets out.
Nothing stirs.
Dogs don't even wag their tails.
Quiet.
Still.
Boring.

That's Ashland—
The Best Little Town in Florida.
At least that's what the sign at the city limits says.

We order out for pizza:
        Large pepperoni.
        Medium cheese.

Man on the phone says,
Leave the money on the porch.

We do.
I put a rock on top of the cash.
So it doesn't blow away.

An hour later . . .
     Knock-knock-knock.
By the time I get to the door,
two pizza boxes replace the money.
The rock
sits on
top of
them.

Delivery guy runs down the driveway,
all the way to his car.
Like he thinks he can catch something
through   the   walls.

As I turn to come back in,
I see it.

More graffiti, Momma,
I say, closing the door on Ashland,
The Best Little Town in Florida.

7

***Calvin! Phone!* Momma hollers from the kitchen.**

Who is it?

Izzy.

My heart s - k - i - p - s three beats.
Bikini thoughts flash through my brain.
My face feels hot.
Then I remember I'm a liar.
My brain tells my feet:

> Move.
> Walk to the kitchen.
> Answer the phone.
> Talk to your best friend.

They don't.
I don't.
Instead, words slide up from my throat,
pushing against my teeth,
out between my lips.

> *Tell her I'll call her back.*

No response.

Momma appears at the bedroom door.
I'll do no such thing.
Go talk to her.

My hot face is gone.
So are the bikini thoughts.
Both replaced by an uneasiness.
I move in slow motion
to the kitchen.
Pick up the phone.
>*Hello?*

>>*Hey, Poet Boy. How's it going?*

Thoughts ping-pong inside me.
There's a million ways to answer that.
I want to tell her everything.
And I want to keep everything a secret.
I want everything to stay exactly the same.
And I want things to be different.

>*Good.*
>I lie.
>*Just fine.*
>*We had pizza for lunch.*
>How dumb.

>>*Ooookay.*
>>Izzy knows it's dumb, too.
>>*The turtles hatched.*

She'll understand,
my brain tells me.
No, she'll hate me.
A different part of my brain warns.
She has boobs.
Where did that come from?

What?

The turtles. They hatched.

    Great.
    My face is red again.
    Embarrassed.
    Me thinking about bikinis.
    Izzy talking about turtles.

Gramps found 'em last night. Came and got me.
Got there in time to see the last ones
in the first nest digging out of the sand.

I want to say:
Izzy, I'm sick.
I don't say anything.

I've seen it—we've seen it—
a million times, but it's still amazing.
Their flippers working to push the sand away.
Poking their heads into the night air.
The pile of wiggling turtles,

maybe a hundred of them,
squirming together.

I want to say:
All three of us are sick.
We've got HIV.
That's why . . . the other night . . .
when we were talking . . .
I don't say anything.

And they start moving—
crawling across the beach,
inch-by-inch all the way to the water.
How do they know to do that?
I know it's instinctive. But how?
How do they know how to survive?
How to get to the water?
How to find home?

I want to say:
It's terminal.
No way to survive.
No treatment.
We're gonna die, Izzy.
There's nothing we can do about it.
I don't say anything.

Who knows? But they do.
Each one, all by itself,
heading straight to the water

with only the moonlight to show the way.
It's like the waves are calling to them, or something.
And then a few reach the edge of the water,
and put their toes in for the first time,
and the next wave washes them out from the beach.

I want to say:
They kicked us out of church,
and out of school.
That's why Momma's homeschooling us.
But the judge has said we can go back.
They have to let us back in school.
I don't say anything.

Their flippers start paddling like
they've done it all their lives.
Well, I guess they have done it all their lives—
even though their lives just started.

I want to say:
I'm scared, Izzy.
Terrified.
I don't say anything.

Calvin? You there?

      Yep.

You've not said a word.

Sounds cool, Izzy.
Wish I'd been there.

Yeah, it was cool. We just got in.
Me and Gramps spent all night at the beach.
The second nest started hatching out about an hour later.
As soon as we walked in the door, I wanted to tell you all
about it.

All night?
Just walked in?
Maybe that means no cruller and coffee.
          Maybe that means no newspaper.
                    Maybe that means no AP story.
                              Maybe that means my secret's still
                              a secret.

Listen, she says.
We need to talk.

Maybe.
          Maybe not.
I don't want to risk it.
I can't take the chance.
If we don't talk about it, then—
well, then nothing will change.

                    Hey, Izzy, I say.
                    I gotta go.
                    Can I call you back?

Sure. When?

Later.

Okay.

We say goodbye.
Me first.
We hang up.
Me first.

I won't, of course.
        Call her back, I mean.

Can we live at the beach?

Charlie asks
    out of the middle of nowhere.

Thoughts of bikinis pop into my brain—again.
A tingle runs through me.
I fight back a smile.
And blush, of course.
I won't talk to Izzy.
But I can't stop thinking about her.

Momma shakes her head.

    We'll go to the beach
    Labor Day weekend.
    Now we gotta get ready for school.

Labor Day weekend might as well be
a million days away.
A million long school days away.

If you ask me,
there's not much to getting ready for school.
Pencils and paper from Dollar City.

Two bucks for each of us.
That'd do it.

> *We've got school supplies to buy,*
> Momma says, like she's reading my mind,
> *Pencils, paper, book bags . . .*

Momma, Charlie interrupts,
They're called backpacks.

> *Okay then, pencils, paper, backpacks, new jeans,*
> *socks, underwear . . .*

Who's gonna be looking at our underwear?

> *All three of you need haircuts.*

It'll grow back in no time.

> *You're going back to school, and you need to look*
> *your best.*

For who?
No one's gonna care.
No one's even gonna look.

But that's the kind of thing a momma bird worries about.

Our momma worries a lot.
She worries for two.

For as long as we can remember,
she's been Momma and Daddy.

I couldn't make Daddy stay.
No matter how hard I tried.
And I tried—as much as a kid can—
until I stopped trying,
and he left for good.
That's when Dutch and Tiny
told me—
their oldest grandson—
I was the new
man of the family.
And I've tried—
as much as a kid can—
but I guess I've not tried hard enough
since Momma's given
that job to Curtis.

Since we got the letters,
Momma's been
our Momma,
our Daddy,
our nurse,
our cook,
our preacher,
our teacher.

But, honestly,
Momma doesn't know squat about teaching.

She tried keeping three boys in
the house all day,
five days a week.

That didn't work.

She tried teaching reading, math, science,
social studies, cursive writing, poetry,
and anything else she could think of.

Most of that didn't work either.

I ended up helping Charlie with reading and writing.
Curtis helped him with math.
Charlie got the hang of it real easy.
He even started making up his own equations.

2 + 1 = My brothers and me, he said.
3 + 1 (the 1's for Momma) = The Johnstons.
4 – 100 = Us without the beach.

I wish there was an equation
to solve the Izzy problem.
I wish that everything in Ashland
would add up to something good.
I hope that HIV
won't divide us,
or worse,
subtract one of us from the
Johnston family equation.

Right now everything's like a
math word problem where you
can't figure out what you're
even supposed to do,
let alone
find the
answer.

DAY 3
MONDAY
AUGUST 17, 1987

1

I've never seen so many mad people.

Angry.
Annoyed.
Bitter.
Enraged.
Furious.
Heated.
Hostile.
Indignant.
Irate.
Irritable.
Offended.
Outraged.
Resentful.
Sullen.

Hacked off. Like I thought.

2

Their anger can't fit in the gym.

The School Board decided to meet
in the high school gymnasium.
They wanna have enough seats.

They *don't* have enough seats.

We're up front—front row.
    Momma,
        the lawyer,
            Curtis,
                Charlie,
                    and me.

The School Board members—
all eight—
sit at a table on the stage.

I recognize two of them.
Mr. Perkins from Open Door Fellowship,
and some woman I've
seen at the bank.

The crowd's too much
for the air conditioner.
People fan themselves.
And sweat.

The place is loud
with rumbling voices,
crying babies,
shouts and
jeers,
squeaky bleachers,
clanking metal chairs.

Familiar sounds.
But together, they
seem unfamiliar.
Foreign.
As if my body has
been plucked up
from home and
dropped into
a new country.
A strange land
where I don't know
the language.
Or the people.
Or their customs.

Maybe shouts and jeers
are how they

welcome guests here.
Maybe signs are, too.

There are lots of signs.
Lots and lots of signs.
Plastered on walls.
Gripped in sweaty white-knuckled fists.
Waved in the air so everyone sees them.

NOT IN OUR TOWN.

KEEP OUR KIDS SAFE.

AIDS KILLS.

My body is suddenly
plopped back into
Ashland, Florida.
Not some
foreign country.
I know the language.
And the people.
And the customs.
It's all familiar.
Too familiar.
I wish I didn't know what any of it meant.
I wish I could be a tourist heading home after a
quick visit.

Our names aren't on any of the signs,
but they might as well be.
Why don't the natives of Ashland
go ahead and say it—

GET OUT CHARLIE!

NO MORE CURTIS!

WE HATE CALVIN!

JOHNSTONS = DEATH

It is a strange land.
A strange, familiar land.

3

THUD! THUD! THUD!

I jerk and look over at Curtis,
thinking he's making sound effects again—
maybe shooting down the enemies in the crowd.

There's never gonna be enough *rat-a-tat-tats* for that.

It's Mr. Perkins.
Pounding a gavel.
Wipes sweat from his forehead.

Meeting's called to order.
> *Things are pretty much not in order.*

Roll call of members.
> *They're sitting at a table. How hard could that be?*

The pledge.
> *At least I know this part.*

Approval of minutes.
> *Why do they call notes, minutes?*

Time for new business.
> *Finally.*

Seems like a lot of work to say,
> *Let's talk about those*
> *Johnston boys going to school.*

—or—

> *Let's talk about those Johnston boys*
> *NOT going to school.*

Mr. Perkins clears his throat.
> *Our new business for tonight:*
> *HIV and AIDS in School.*

Shouts ring out:
NO!

    NO!

        NO!

            Our kids won't go!

Hands pick up the rhythm:

Clap!

    Clap!

        Clap!

            Clap-clap. Clap! Clap!

Then feet:

Stomp!
    Stomp!
        Stomp!
            Stomp-stomp. Stomp! Stomp!

The crowd noise doubles, triples.

NO!
    NO!
        NO!
            OUR KIDS WON'T GO!

Curtis sits on the edge of his seat—
looking around.
Fists balled up.
Ready for a fight.

Charlie pushes himself deep
into Momma's side,
trying to disappear.

Fight or flight.
Momma taught us that in science.
It's instinctive.
Since the beginning of time.
Part of survival.

Fight = Curtis.
Flight = Charlie.

But there's a third category.
That category's
reserved
for
guys
||||&
me.

Freeze.

I read about it in the encyclopedia.
Some animals flee—
run for their lives.
Others put up a fight.
If they're gonna die,
they're gonna die on their own terms.

The third group freezes.
They
            stand
                        there
                                    and let whatever's gonna happen,
                                                    happen.

That's me.
Mr. Freeze.
Mr. Winter Blast.

Mr. Butt-Stuck-to-his-Chair.

Flight might save your life.
Fighting might, too.
Freezing?
Dead in the water.
Every time.

But frozen can also mean—
                Suspended in time.
                        In a preserved state.
                                Staying exactly the same.
So frozen might not be so bad after all,
Even if it does mean
dead in the water.
Every time.

4

Order! Order!

Momma puts a hand on Curtis' shoulder,

THUD!
      THUD!
            THUD!

holds it there, 'til his body relaxes.

THUD!
      THUD!
            THUD!

He slumps back in the chair.

THUD!
      THUD!
            THUD!

Charlie still huddles deep into her side.

THUD!
      THUD!
            THUD!

Mr. Freeze is frozen.

Mr. Perkins says.
We want to listen to each other.

     We do?

Let's treat each other with respect.

     Too late for that.

Consider the best interest of the children.

     Yours?
     Theirs?
     Us?

The first speaker is the Atlanta CDC man.
He steps up to the podium on the stage.
Speaking on behalf of the Johnstons,
Mr. Perkins says, just like the newspaper.

We don't need someone to speak for us.
We've got Momma.
We've got a lawyer.
Why do we need this stranger standing up
pretending he's here on our behalf,
like we invited him or something?
I fold my arms across my chest.
Slide down in my chair.

Ready to tune him out.

The man is big,
tall,
barrel chested,
navy blue suit,
red bow tie,
gray hair,
white beard.
Like Santa Claus got dressed up.

The heat doesn't
seem to bother him.
Not one bit.
The shouts don't either.
And neither do the signs.

His voice booms through the microphone.
Tells how you get HIV, and
               how you don't.

               Not from mosquito bites.
               Not from kissing.
               Not from using the same toilet.
               Not by holding hands.
               Not by sharing a toothbrush.
               Not by going to school together.

It's stuff we've heard before.
It's mostly stuff people in Ashland have never heard before.
It's all stuff I wish Izzy could hear before we're not
friends for the rest of our lives.

> *The treatment of the Johnstons . . .*
> Mr. CDC man continues
> *. . . a tragedy . . .*
> *. . . injustice . . .*
> *. . . they pose no credible threat . . .*

I sit up taller.
Unfold my arms.

This man is talking about *me*.
Talking *for* me.
On our behalf.
On *my* behalf.

Who does that?
No one I know.
Not even me.

5

He reaches out his hand to shake mine.

The Atlanta CDC man is finished talking.
He's walked off the stage.

The audience is polite.
They clap
                        a little.

He shakes
Momma's hand.
Then Charlie's,
down the line to Curtis,
then he steps over to me.

A man's handshake,
Dutch told me,
shows his character.

A man with a firm handshake,
a man who looks you in the eye,
that's a man you can trust.

No one's touched me since I got it.
No one except
Momma,
     and the doctors,
          and the nurses.

Doctors and nurses
     only touch me
          if they're wearing gloves.

I've been thinking no one will ever touch me again.
     No high-fives after a good game—
     if I'm ever on a team again.
          No handshake at graduation—
          if I ever graduate.
               No hand holding with a
               girlfriend—
               if I ever have one.

I probably wouldn't
touch me either.

Mr. CDC man is holding out his hand.
His bare hand.

I stretch out my arm.
He grips my hand—firm and strong,
looks me in the eye,
puts his other hand on my shoulder.

I look him straight in the eye.
Shake back, firm and strong.

Our skin touches.
Palm against palm.
Fingers lock around hands.
His hand is big.
Strong.
Warm.

He's. Not. Afraid
        of germs,
        of HIV,
        of AIDS,
        of me.

It gives me a warm feeling—
like sitting on Santa's lap when
you're a kid, or something.

The CDC man turns, walks back up on stage,

reaches out his hand to Mr. Perkins.

Mr. Perkins
       does not
              reach back.

No one does.
None of them.
No one shakes the man's hand.

Came all the way from Atlanta, Georgia,
and not one single School Board member shakes his
hand.

I know why.
They know why.
The CDC man knows why.
Everyone knows why.

The man from Atlanta was
the one and only pro
of the pros and cons.
No one else
      speaks
          for
               us.
                  For
                     me.

7

That's Rev. Walker,

Charlie whispers.
Rev. Otis Walker is at the microphone.
His wife stands beside him.
So does Daniel, his son.
We used to play on the same little league team.
Went on scouting camp outs together.
Hung out at church camp 'round a fire.

> *Now, I don't mean any offense,* Rev. Walker says.
> *I'm sure the Johnstons are nice enough folks.*

You know us.

> *But I don't want*
> *Those kids with my son.*
> *It's not safe.*
> *Not healthy.*
> *Plain and simple.*

Simple all right.
Simpleminded.

He's a fool, Curtis mutters.
They're all fools.

I look at Momma.
She doesn't say anything.
Rocks back and forth,
                back and forth.
                        back and forth.

500 against 3.

PAAS—
            Parents
            Against
            AIDS
            in
            School—
has 500 members.
They signed a petition.
Rev. Walker is their spokesperson.

The 500 voices say—
            Who's gonna clean up their blood?
            Can you guarantee no one will get it?
            Do our kids have to sit with them?
                Talk with them?
                        Share with them?
                                Eat with them?
                                        Play with them?

Test everyone for HIV and AIDS.
Identify the carriers.
Give the sick ones their own schools.
Let them go to school—but not our school.
Keep them away from our kids.

Let 'em talk, boys.
Momma says, in the middle of her rocking.
Let 'em talk all they want.
We're starting school next week,
come hell, or high water.

That's the closest to cussing
Momma's ever come.

Rev. Walker's not the end of it.
The people of Ashland
want all their voices
to be heard.

We hear each of them.
Every single one.

I sit frozen
wondering if the fire of their words
might melt me.

NO! NO! NO! Our kids won't go! NO! NO! NO! Our kids won't go!
NO! NO! NO! Our kids won't go! NO! NO! NO! Our kids won't go!
NO! NO! NO! Our kids won't go! NO! NO! NO! Our kids won't go!
NO! NO! NO! Our kids won't go! NO! NO! NO! Our kids won't go!
NO! NO! NO! Our kids won't go! NO! NO! NO! Our kids won't go!
NO! NO! NO! Our kids won't go! NO! NO! NO! Our kids won't go!
NO! NO! NO! Our kids won't go! NO! NO! NO! Our kids won't go!
NO! NO! NO! Our kids won't go! NO! NO! NO! Our kids won't go!
NO! NO! NO! Our kids won't go! NO! NO! NO! Our kids won't go!
NO! NO! NO! Our kids won't go! NO! NO! NO! Our kids won't go!
NO! NO! NO! Our kids won't go! NO! NO! NO! Our kids won't go!
NO! NO! NO! Our kids won't go! NO! NO! NO! Our kids won't go!
NO! NO! NO! Our kids won't go! NO! NO! NO! Our kids won't go!
NO! NO! NO! Our kids won't go! NO! NO! NO! Our kids won't go!
NO! NO! NO! Our kids won't go! NO! NO! NO! Our kids won't go!
NO! NO! NO! Our kids won't go! NO! NO! NO! Our kids won't go!
NO! NO! NO! Our kids won't go! NO! NO! NO! Our kids won't go!
NO! NO! NO! Our kids won't go! NO! NO! NO! Our kids won't go!
NO! NO! NO! Our kids won't go! NO! NO! NO! Our kids won't go!
NO! NO! NO! Our kids won't go! NO! NO! NO! Our kids won't go!
NO! NO! NO! Our kids won't go! NO! NO! NO! Our kids won't go!
NO! NO! NO! Our kids won't go! NO! NO! NO! Our kids won't go!
NO! NO! NO! Our kids won't go! NO! NO! NO! Our kids won't go!
NO! NO! NO! Our kids won't go! NO! NO! NO! Our kids won't go!

NO! NO! NO! Our kids won't go! NO! NO! NO! Our kids won't go!
NO! NO! NO! Our kids won't go! NO! NO! NO! Our kids won't go!
NO! NO! NO! Our kids won't go! NO! NO! NO! Our kids won't go!
NO! NO! NO! Our kids won't go! NO! NO! NO! Our kids won't go!
NO! NO! NO! Our kids won't go! NO! NO! NO! Our kids won't go!
NO! NO! NO! Our kids won't go! NO! NO! NO! Our kids won't go!
NO! NO! NO! Our kids won't go! NO! NO! NO! Our kids won't go!
NO! NO! NO! Our kids won't go! NO! NO! NO! Our kids won't go!
NO! NO! NO! Our kids won't go! NO! NO! NO! Our kids won't go!
NO! NO! NO! Our kids won't go! NO! NO! NO! Our kids won't go!
NO! NO! NO! Our kids won't go! NO! NO! NO! Our kids won't go!
NO! NO! NO! Our kids won't go! NO! NO! NO! Our kids won't go!
NO! NO! NO! Our kids won't go! NO! NO! NO! Our kids won't go!
NO! NO! NO! Our kids won't go! NO! NO! NO! Our kids won't go!
NO! NO! NO! Our kids won't go! NO! NO! NO! Our kids won't go!
NO! NO! NO! Our kids won't go! NO! NO! NO! Our kids won't go!
NO! NO! NO! Our kids won't go! NO! NO! NO! Our kids won't go!
NO! NO! NO! Our kids won't go! NO! NO! NO! Our kids won't go!
NO! NO! NO! Our kids won't go! NO! NO! NO! Our kids won't go!
NO! NO! NO! Our kids won't go! NO! NO! NO! Our kids won't go!
NO! NO! NO! Our kids won't go! NO! NO! NO! Our kids won't go!
NO! NO! NO! Our kids won't go! NO! NO! NO! Our kids won't go!
NO! NO! NO! Our kids won't go! NO! NO! NO! Our kids won't go!
NO! NO! NO! Our kids won't go! NO! NO! NO! Our kids won't go!
NO! NO! NO! Our kids won't go! NO! NO! NO! Our kids won't go!
NO! NO! NO! Our kids won't go! NO! NO! NO! Our kids won't go!
NO! NO! NO! Our kids won't go! NO! NO! NO! Our kids won't go!
NO! NO! NO! Our kids won't go! NO! NO! NO! Our kids won't go!
NO! NO! NO! Our kids won't go! NO! NO! NO! Our kids won't go!
NO! NO! NO! Our kids won't go! NO! NO! NO! Our kids won't go!

I didn't think things could get worse,

They do. At the house.

Ripped open trash bags,
      thrown in the yard,
surround us with the odor of
      rotten eggs,
          spoiled meat,
             dirty diapers.

Yesterday's graffiti,
covered with new graffiti.

AIDS SUCKS!
GET OUT OF TOWN!
NO! NO! NO!

The rest of the red words
d
  r
    i
      p,

d
  r
    i
      p,
d
  r
    i
      p
        p
          i
            n
              g

down the walls
could help fill the
Cuss Jar.

We'll take care of everything, Momma, I say.
We'll get everything back to normal.

> *Normal, Momma repeats.*
> *Nothing's normal about any of this.*

She's right of course.
But cleaning up the yard,
and scrubbing down the walls
will get things back looking normal.
Maybe.
Like nothing ever happened.
Kind of.

Like nothing ever changed.
Sort of.

    Sometimes I want to be a plate spinner,
    like the one I saw at the county fair.
    Keeping everything balanced. Steady.
    Keeping everything from crashing down.

    I'd spin some plates in one direction,
    trying to turn things back to the way
    they used to be—like cleaning paint off the house.
    I'd spin more plates the opposite direction,
    trying to move things forward to get them
    into some kind of new balance—
    like going to school.

    The man at the carnival made it look easy.
    Moving back and forth between the plates.
    Gently rotating the stick under a wobbly one.
    Or quickly sliding a hand across a plate's rim to
    keep it spinning.
    At the end of the show,
    he caught each plate,
    one on top of the other—
        Clink. Clink. Clink. Clink.
    Without one slip.
    Without one shattered plate.

    I'm no plate spinner.
    I'm Mr. Freeze.

Momma gets Charlie to bed.
Tries to sleep herself.

Curtis and I go outside
to pick up garbage,
and to wash Ashland
off our house.

10

Rinnngggg.

I yank up the receiver.

Hello?

   Calvin?

Yeah.

   It's Izzy.

Hey.

Wish I'd not answered.
Wrap the phone cord
round and round my arm.
Rest my forehead against the refrigerator.

   I thought you were going to call me back.
   We need to talk.

My forehead taps the refrigerator.
Once.
Twice.
Three times.
I breathe in through my nose.
Hold it.
And hold my thoughts inside, too.
She read the article.
She knows everything.
Everything about us.
Everything about me.
Everything.
She knows.
She knows.
She knows.
I breathe out.

I read the article.

Of course you did.
I think it.
Don't say it.
Everything.
She knows.
Everything.

Calvin . . .

It's not a good time.
It's late.

We've got a mess here.

I talk fast.
Cord presses into my skin.
My arm turns red.
Forehead taps against the avocado-colored Frigidaire
again
and again
and again.

Momma's trying to get Charlie to sleep.
We went to a meeting.
The school board.
It was bad.
Real bad.
A CDC man was there
He shook our hands.
My hand.
Cool. Right?

      Calvin.

I really gotta go. I'll call you.

      Promise?

Sure. Of course. Promise.

Click.

I have no idea which way to spin this wobbly plate.
No idea how to keep it balanced.
No clue whether to spin forward,
            or spin back,
                    to keep things the same.
Something has changed.
I'm afraid it's changed forever.

CRASH!

1

Curtis lands a karate chop, spins, kicks.
Charlie crawls away under the chairs, between
stomping feet.
I'm in a penguin suit, sitting on a block of ice.

Thud. Thud. Thud.

I dream about it all night.
The meeting. The gavel.
The dream grows bigger . . .
into a nightmare, and then
some kung-fu movie
with sub-titles.

Thud. Thud. Thud.

Each scene is
weirder than the one before.

But all the scenes
have two things
in common.
> #1—Anger.
> #2—Hate.

Just like the meeting.

Thud. Thud. Thud.

I open my eyes.
Light peeks around the edges of the
sheet that covers the window.

I stretch.
Charlie's arm dangles from the top bunk.
Curtis snores from the air mattress on the floor.

Thud. Thud. Thud.

It's the door.
Someone's knocking.

I swing my legs out of bed,
pull on my jeans,
step over Curtis,
head down the hall.

I jump and kick
karate-style
with my right leg,

just like Curtis did
in the dream.
I fall, face-first.
Leave the fighting
to the fighter, I mumble
into the shag carpet.

Thud! Thud! Thud!

Coming, I say all hoarse-like,
pushing myself up from the floor.

Click. Old deadbolt.
Click. New deadbolt.

Crack the door open,
chain still on.

Heat and humidity
seep through the crack,
press on my chest.
The chest
that covers the heart
that pumps the blood
that everyone's so worried about.

A woman on the porch—
holding a clipboard, camera around her neck.
Probably doesn't know she's at HIV House.

Good morning, she says.
I'm Mandy Kissinger.

I stare.
Am I supposed to know her?

From the newspaper.

I stare.
Is she selling papers door-to-door?
I'm sure we don't have money for that.

I want to interview your
Mom about school . . .
and the meeting . . .
and you boys.
You must be Calvin, the oldest one.

I stare.
An interview?
With Momma?
About us?

Can I talk to your mom?

Wait here, I say.

I close the door.
Click. New deadbolt.
Click. Old deadbolt.

Head down the hall.

Momma's favorite song
drifts under her bedroom door.

> *Through the storm we reach the shore*
> *You gave it all but I want more*
> *And I'm waiting for you*
> *With or without you*
>
> *With or without you*
> *I can't live*
> *With or without you*

I've never understood that song.
Who's it talking about?
And who does Momma think it's about?
Who can't she live with or without?
Daddy?
She can live without him—I'm pretty sure.
Us boys?
She can live with us—I think.
Probably not easy though.
Can she live without us?
Bet she doesn't wanna find out.
I don't either.

I throw another karate kick,
this time without the jump.
Success.

Knock. Knock.

Momma?

2

Mandy Kissinger's still standing there.

A reporter at our front door.
That's never happened before.

She's getting ready, I explain.

Mandy Kissinger nods her head.
Stands there. Looking down at her clipboard.

Do you write AP stories?

> *Not yet.*
> *Never made it that big.*

Good.

Whatever Momma tells
this woman, won't go any
further than Ashland, Florida.
I can live with that.
(Though I'd rather live without it.)

> *There's a box out here,* she says,
> looking down at the porch.

Does it have dirty diapers or dog poop in it?
I ask, looking down, too.

> *Looks like groceries.*

Cans, bags, and cartons
stick out of a cardboard box.
I step out.
Pick up the box.

Come in, Mandy Kissinger.

3

Charlie wears superhero underwear.

Hardly anyone knows that.
Mandy Kissinger knows it now.
There's a headline for her.

Charlie races out of the living room
once he finished scratching and yawning,
and opens his eyes and
sees her.

Truth is, he doesn't
just wear superhero underwear.
He's even got a cape somewhere.

And he doesn't just wear the stuff,
he wants to *be* a superhero.
Actually, he wants to be Superman.
        The Man of Steel.
                The man who can outrun trains,
                        leap buildings with a single bound,
                                stop a speeding bullet.

Curtis used to want to be the Hulk.
Still never misses a rerun on TV.
I can't ever see him being seven feet tall,
or having bulging muscles, or being green,
but he does have the temper for it.

I'm into J'onn J'onzz
(AKA: Martian Hunter).
He's part of the new
Justice League International.
The guy has like ten super powers.
The writers invent one whenever
J'onn J'onzz needs one.
Need to get somewhere fast?
Bang! You can fly.
Need to sneak into a room?
Voila! You're invisible.
Need to recover from an injury?
Boom! You have self-healing powers.
Now that's a superhero.

I guess every kid wants to be a Super Hero.
Who doesn't want to save the world?
But there's a flip side, too.
Every superhero comes with an archenemy—
        a Joker,
        a Penguin,
        a General Zod
                —a nemesis to defeat over and over.

Rev. Walker may be our archenemy.
Or the school board.
Or maybe everyone in PAAS—all 500 of them.

If this was a new edition of Justice League International,
we'd win the battle against our nemesis,
but another one would be right around the corner.

Charlie's
underwear
and cape
wouldn't
change
a thing.

4

Momma's still not presentable.

Charlie and Curtis are.
At least their bottom halves are.

They sort through the box.
     Soup.
          Chef Boyardee.
               Mixed vegetables.
     Bread.
          Mac and cheese.
               Vienna sausages.
     Tuna.
          Peanut butter.
               A card.

Johnstons written on the envelope.
I rip it open,
pull out the card.
Money floats to the floor.

Sixty bucks! Curtis whoops,
scooping up the bills.

I read the card out loud—

> You still have friends in Ashland.
> We're sorry for all your troubles.

Mandy Kissinger writes on her clipboard.

The card's not signed.
I guess that means
our *friends* don't want
anyone knowing they're our friends.
Not even us.

What good are anonymous friends?
What do we do if we need something?
Call an anonymous phone number?
Knock on an anonymous door?
Go to an anonymous church?

Do these people think some boxes and cans,
a card and sixty bucks
somehow shows
us they're
our friends?
Seriously?
They can't even sign
their names
on a card.
Doesn't
sound

like a
friend
to
me.

At least not one worth having.

5

Mandy Kissinger asks a lot of questions.

The boys' ages and school grades?
Who's their doctor?
How did you find out?
When did you get the diagnosis?
What was it like to homeschool three boys?
Why did you take the case to court?
Did you think you stood a chance?
How did you feel about the judge's ruling?

I sit crossed legged on the floor listening.
Curtis and Charlie bang around in the kitchen.
Doors slam. Pots clank. Boxes are ripped open.

I get bored.
Go to the mailbox.
Junk mail.
Bills.
A letter.
Addressed to me.

I know it's from Izzy.
Who else would send me a letter?

Not that she ever has before.
I don't wanna read it.
I don't wanna think about it.
I shove the envelope in my pocket.

Back inside, Mandy's still asking questions—
What are your plans after last night's meeting?
How are you getting ready for school?
What's the prognosis?

Momma clips off answers.
She stops after the last question.
Prognosis? she repeats. *For school?*

Mandy looks at me.
Then back at Momma.
For the boys, she says softly.

Why don't you just ask *it*, Mandy Kissinger?
Just say it—
Are they
gonna live
or
die?

Momma looks toward the kitchen.
Momma bird checking the nest.
Curtis is sitting on the counter eating cereal from a box.

Charlie's on a stepstool shoveling mac and cheese into
his mouth.
She's wondering if they're listening.
If they can hear.
She may be wondering if they know.
If she should tell them.

Momma look straight at me.
I suck in a deep breath,
and let it out.
My lips tighten
together.
I nod.
I don't know why.
Am I telling her I know?
Am I saying it's okay to talk about it?

I lean against the wall.
Its coolness pushes
goosebumps
up along
my
spine.

I look at Momma.
Her eyes are wet.
Filling up with tears.
Don't do it, Momma,
I wanna say.
Don't cry.

She hardly ever lets anyone
see her cry.
No matter how bad
things are.
She's too private
for that.
Too strong.
Don't cry, Momma.
Don't cry.
I repeat the words
over and over
in my brain.

Momma looks back at Mandy Kissinger.
She can't hold it back.
A dam breaks.
Tears roll out of Momma's eyes,
over her cheeks,
streaking toward
her jaw.

She doesn't wipe them away.
They roll
one
      after
           another.
A tidal wave.
Tear after tear after tear after tear.

She's not let us see her cry once.

Not when we got the diagnosis.
Not when we got the letter from school.
Not when nasty words were painted on the house.
Not when she lost her job.
Not when her sorry boyfriend left us.
Haven't seen her cry since Dutch's funeral,
and before that, Tiny's funeral.

But she does cry.
She thinks with the door closed
and the music up loud
no one can
hear her.
I can.
I never know what to do,
So I close our bedroom door,
cover my ears with a pillow.
Sometimes
I cry
too.

But *seeing* her cry is different.
I want to look away.
But I can't.
There's a pain in my chest.
Like I'm hurting for her.
And my own tears begin
to flood out of my eyes.
It hurts bad to see Momma cry.
It hurts real bad.

I don't talk about death, she finally tells Mandy Kissinger.
I concentrate on what I can do something about.
I can't do nothing about death.

Momma's hands wipe at her cheeks.
She lifts the sleeve of her T-shirt
to mop them away.

Her still-wet eyes
look back in the kitchen.
I can see them move as she looks
at Charlie, then up at Curtis,
then over to me.
Looking at her boys
that she can't do nothing about.

6

Do you boys have anything to say?

Momma asks.

Mandy is snapping pictures
of the living room,
the kitchen,
the box of food.
Charlie's in Momma's lap,
Curtis and me shirtless on the sofa.

Curtis shakes his head.
Charlie looks at his empty bowl.
Mandy Kissinger lowers her camera.
She and Momma look at me.

Me—Mr. Frozen-in-one-spot.

I shrug.

> *We just wanna be,* Curtis finally says,
> *like everybody else.*

7

My cousin has it . . .

Mandy Kissinger says
at the front door,
turning to look at Momma.
Momma looks back to see who's listening.
No one is.
Except me,
like always.

AIDS, I mean.
He left home.
Moved to New York City.
Came back to Tampa this year. Sick.
Real sick. People have been awful.
Just awful. Even his mom and dad.
He's still my cousin, Ms. Johnston.
Just like always. Nothing's changed.

Even his mom and dad.
The words hit me between the eyes.
Got HIV and even his mom treats him awful.
He's like one of those guys in the
news magazines in the stacks
at the Ashland City Library.

Alone.
Wanting to live.
Waiting to die.

Momma hugs her.
Walks her out to the front porch.

Nothing's changed, the reporter says again.

I bet Mandy Kissinger's
cousin doesn't think
nothing's changed.
Neither do I.

My hand has reached into my pocket a dozen times.

Touching the envelope.
Feeling guilty for not opening it.

I lock myself in the bathroom.
Close the toilet lid.
Sit down.
Tear open the envelope.
Pull out the paper.
Unfold it.

Calvin,

*I read the article. I don't care. I mean, of course I care.
About you. About Curtis and Charlie. About you having
HIV. About you being healthy. But none of that changes
us, or you. Nothing's changed, Calvin. We're friends like
always, like we've always been, and we always will be.
I'm sorry for the crap I said about people who get AIDS.
That was stupid. Real stupid.*

Love,
Izabelle

I fold the letter.
Tear it in half.
Then tear it again,

    and again,

        and again.

Same with the envelope.
Open the toilet lid.
Toss in the shreds.
Flush.

You're better off without me, Izabelle.
Because *everything* has changed.

1

More graffiti.

Red paint splatters the walls.
Lots of bad spellers in Ashland.
Maybe going to public school's
not such a great idea.

Scrubbing the walls didn't work.
The words were still there.
Fainter.
Faded.
But there.
Like nasty whispers behind our backs.
Like angry stares from passing cars.
Like hate hidden behind fake smiles.

Now layers of words cover the walls.
Old, faint-whispered words.
New, loud-shouted words.
Like a crowd of Ashland's finest
outside our front door

calling out to us
day and night.

Today, the four of us paint over the words.
Sun shines warm on my bare shoulders.
I like the feel of the muscles in my arms as
they contract with each swipe of the paint roller.
It feels good to paint over the ugliness.
To get things looking right again.

There's only one problem.

The words
          b-l-e-e-d
                    through.

You can't hide hate, Momma says.
Can't cover it up.
Ugliness shows up one way or the other.

She's right.
Hate bleeds through
                    as much as a hemophilic with a bad cut.
No hiding it.
And even if you could—
                    hide it, I mean—
                              it would still be there.
Below the surface.
There's no stopping it.

Mandy Kissinger promised
the article would be in today's paper.
I pick up the morning edition at the laundromat.
No article.
Don't know why I thought there would be.
Why I believed her.
Why I thought anyone would
want to read a story about us anyway.

Okay, I do know why.
Because I *wanted* to believe her.
And I *wanted* people to know the truth.
Even if it makes me feel worse than naked.
Somehow I thought—I think—those black-inked words—
        the ones I thought would be in the newspaper—
            would cover up . .
                take away . . .
                    erase . . .
                            the words
                            painted on our
                            house.
I hoped the true words, the ones in black,
could cover the red words
so
they
never
could
bleed
through
again.

2

That's ridiculous, Fred, and you know it.

Momma's on the phone.
Her voice is quiet, slow.
Like it gets when she's mad.

> My mind is flipping through names.
> Fred?

I'm telling you, there's nothing to worry about.
Nothing.
Trust me.

> Some relative?
> Nobody I remember.

Silence.
She listens.
Yeah.

> An old boyfriend?
> A possibility.

Paces the kitchen.
Uh-huh.

Wipes the counter.
Right.
Piles dishes in the sink.

> Someone from town?
> Someone from church?
> No way.

Of course.
I understand.
We'll honor your wishes.
But this is wrong, Fred.
Silence.
> Whoever Fred is,
> He's got Momma mad.
> Real mad.

She nods.
I understand.

She hangs up.
No goodbye.
Storms off to her room.
Slams the door.
Turns Abba up—full blast.

Still don't know who Fred is.
One thing is pretty clear—
> whoever he is,
> he's been added to Momma's don't-like list.

Momma drives us up to Tampa.

We've got sixty bucks to spend.
We buy school clothes.
        Clean down to our underwear.
Get haircuts.
        Buzz cuts for everyone.
        Momma was right.
        We do look better.

No one knows us in Tampa.
        They may have read about us.
        But the AP story didn't have photos.
        (Not like Mandy Kissinger's imaginary article.)
It's nice.
Normal.
        No one worried about catching something.
        No one telling us what we can't do.
        No one whispering or pointing.
        No protest signs.
        No graffiti.

We eat at the Wagon Wheel Buffet.
All-you-can-eat.
Six food stations.
First time in a restaurant in more than a year.

Forget moving to the beach, I say.
We need to move next door to the Wagon Wheel Buffet.

What? Charlie yelps.

He's joking, Curtis tells him.

I thought you didn't like change,
Momma says.

This is different.
It's a buffet!

When we get home,
the neighbor's evening paper's
in our driveway.

No article.

Thanks for nothing, Mandy Kissinger.

Calvin, come here.

Momma calls from her bedroom.
Sit down.
She pats the bed.

Fred Lawrence called.

> *Who?*

Izzy's grandfather.

> So that's who Fred is.
> I've always called him *Gramps.*
> Like Izzy always
> called Dutch *Dutch*
> and Tiny *Tiny.*

> *Is everything okay with Izzy?*

Momma nods.
Then shakes her head.

> *What is it Momma?*
> *Tell me.*

Fred says you boys and Izzy can't see each other anymore.

> *What?*
> *Why?*
> I ask.
> But I know why.
>
> Thoughts churn in my brain.
> Gramps can't boss me around.
> He sure can't boss Izzy around.
> He can't tell us not to be friends.
> The whirl in my brain slows down, and the words
> repeat.
> He can't tell us not to be friends.
> He can't tell us not to be friends.
> He can't tell us not to be friends.
>
> No, he can't do that.
> Because
> I
> already
> have.

He read the article in the paper.
He thinks we've been keeping secrets.

> We have.
> But that's because it wasn't important.
> It's not important.
> And we didn't want to worry them.

It doesn't matter.
Izzy even said so in her letter.
This is wrong, Momma, I finally say. Wrong.

We probably should have said something, Momma continues.
Fred said we've been putting Izzy in danger.

> *That's crazy.*
> *I'd never hurt Izzy. Never.*
> *She's my best friend. Was my best friend.*

Momma looks at me, surprised.

> *I'm sick and tired of this.*
> I pound my fist into the mattress.
> *Sick and tired of people telling me what to do.*
> *I'm sick of it Momma.*
> *Everybody pushing me away.*
> *Everybody treating us like we've done something wrong.*
> *Everything changing.*
> *I'm tired of it, Momma, sick and . . .*

For the second time in two days
a tsunami of tears pours from my eyes.
Momma grabs me.
Wraps her arms around me.
Holds me tight.

> *I'm sick of it, Momma, I cry into her shoulder.*
> *Sick of it.*

DAY 6
THURSDAY
AUGUST 20, 1987

1

Don't take one step into that school . . . or else.

A chill runs up my back.
I shiver at the sound of the voice.
Momma, it's another one.

She takes the phone,
holds it to her mouth.

TWEET! TWEEEEEEEEET!

She hangs up.
Acts like it's normal
to blow a whistle
into the phone
at a person
who's
threatening
your
boys.

Not normal for most folks.
        Becoming normal for us.
        At least Momma's trying to pretend that it is.

Mandy Kissinger's article came out this morning.
(It's about time, Mandy Kissinger.)
Front page. Full page.
Big headline.
AIDS COMES TO ASHLAND.
(Was that necessary, Mandy Kissinger?)
Lots of quotes from Momma.
Photos, too.
The box of food.
The three of us shirtless on the couch.
Momma crying.
(That *wasn't* necessary, Mandy Kissinger.)

More reporters showed up.
(It *was* an AP story.)
More reporters is a good thing.
It's not so easy to
paint graffiti on a house,
or dump trash in a yard
when reporters are watching.

So Ashland's finest started calling.

Anonymous calls.
Like the anonymous friends
who didn't sign the card.

For all we know, they're the same people.

We hang up the phone
and it rings again,

        and again,

                and again.

One after another.
The shrill sound makes my ears ring, too.
After the first ten or twelve calls,
Momma found the whistle.
She's been using it ever since.
Blows it. Hangs up. Then goes about her business.

No matter how many calls there've been,
I jump like I've been shot
each time the phone rings.

Anonymous calls.
Feels like the caller is nobody

        and

            everybody

                at the same time.

2

Sometimes they hang up,

and call right back.
Over and over,
I want to yell:

> Who are you?
> What do you want?
> Why won't you leave us alone?

Sometimes they don't
say anything—
breathe into the phone.
That's even creepier.

Some threaten.
Some cuss.
Some name call.

Most are men.
Some women.
A few kids.

They have to be people we know.
Or people who know us.
Or people we've seen in town.
An ocean of people against the four of us.

We're just boys with their momma.
A little island in the Ashland Sea.
Their waves of hate keep roaring towards us.
The tide's rising, threatening to destroy us.
Trying to wash our island away.

Each call gets Momma's *tweet-tweet* treatment.
But that doesn't keep them from calling.

As the day goes on,
the threats,
and the cussing,
and the name calling
get worse.
       Angrier.
          Scarier.

We won't let Charlie answer.
Momma made Curtis stop after he started cussing back
at people.
Sometimes I pick up the receiver and slam it back down.
But the ringing continues.

Unplug the phone, Momma, I say. *Please.*

       No, Momma replies. *I can't.*
       I might need to . . .
       What if . . .
       You boys might . . .
       Fear sweeps across her face.

I see it.
I feel it.
What if one of the anonymous callers
showed up? Then what?
We'd need a phone.
Momma takes a deep breath.
Let it ring.

And it does.
All.
Day.
Long.

After dinner,
when Momma
goes to her room,
closes the door,
and turns Abba up loud,
I sneak into
the kitchen,
pull the cord
from the bottom
of the phone,
lay the receiver
on the counter.

I'm sure we
can survive
one night
without a
phone.

3

There's no scary music.

Like on TV or in the movies.
I'm waiting for it.
Half-a-sleep.

No scary music at all
when I wake up in the middle of the night.

Rub my eyes.
Try to focus.
Then see it.
A shadow.

The street light casts the shadow on the sheet . . .
. . . the sheet on the window . . .
. . . the window of the bedroom . . .
. . . the bedroom where we sleep.

A man.
The shadow is a man.
With something in his hand.

Curtis, I whisper.

Huh? he mumbles
from the air mattress on the floor.

I point.
It takes a second,
but he sees the shadow.
Instantly reaches for a
baseball bat.

No! I say, still whispering.
Go call the . . .
I stop.
The phone.
I unplugged
the phone.

I can hear my panic.
I can taste my fear.
It's that gagging taste you get
before you throw up.

Take Charlie.
Get to Momma's room.
Quick.

Curtis grabs Charlie—still asleep—
from the top bunk and carries him out of the room . . .
. . . the room where we sleep . . .
with a sheet on the window . . .

. . . the window with a man on the other side of it . . .
. . . the man with something in his hand.

Then a
second
shadow
appears.

I slide out of the bunk.
Stand.
Take a step toward the window.
Stop.
Wait.

One shadow leans toward the other,
like they're talking.
The second shadow, points.
The first one nods.
The pointer's shadow disappears.

My mouth is dry.
Hands tremble.
I take another step.

Someone . . . something . . . brushes by my shoulder.
I jump, and make a sound.
A quiet, frightened sound.
Like an animal caught in a trap.

It's Momma.
She heads straight for the window.

Yanks back the sheet.

Who are you, and what the hell are you doing here?
she yells.

I'll get the Cuss Jar,
Curtis says from the doorway,

4

Sorry to disturb you, ma'am.

That's what the police officers say
when they're ready to leave.
They'd gotten a call.
Someone said there were
gunshots
at our
house.

Of course there weren't any gunshots.
Another prank.
Another way to scare us.

The police came to check it out.
They looked around.
Outside first.

Sorry to wake you.
Sorry to scare you.

They look like they are sorry . . .
       . . . sorry they had to come to *our* house.

Lightning flashes off in the distance.

I close the door.
Do the deadbolt routine.
There's another knock.
I do the un-deadbolt routine.
It's one of the cops.
Lopez printed on his badge.

Tell your Momma I'll keep an eye out,
he says.
Then he walks to his patrol car.
Drives away.
I do the deadbolts again.
I almost believe him.

I tell Momma.
Thunder rumbles.
Momma tells us to get to bed.

Curtis goes to our room.
The fighter is *not* scared.

Charlie flees to Momma's room.
The super hero *is* scared.

The freezer sits
in a chair
in the living room.
Wide awake.
Frozen.

5

My hand rests on the phone.

Do I call?
What do I say?
What does it matter?
Just say something, my brain tells me.

Just call.

I plug in the phone.
Lift the receiver.
Hold it against my ear.
Listen to the dial tone.
My hand shakes as
my index finger punches
the first number.
One side of my brain says—*Talk to her.*
The other side says—*Hang up now.*
Area code.
Phone number.
I dial the last number,
take a deep breath—

let it out.

I wait.

    Ring.

A second.

    Ring.

A third.

    Ring.

Hollo?

A man's voice.
Gramps.

I hang up.
Stand there.
Staring at the phone.

I didn't think it through.
Didn't have a plan.
One side of my brain says—*You shouldn't have called.*
The other side says—*Try again.*
Should've thought
she might not answer,
or that he might.
Doesn't matter.
I didn't

      have anything

         to say

           anyway.

Rinnnnnggggg.

My heart skips a beat.
I jerk the phone off the hook.

Izzy . . .

I talk fast.
Before I lose my nerve.
Words pouring out.
Hands shaking.
I'm sorry.
I'm really sorry.
I'm almost breathless.
Like I've run a mile.
I want to talk.
I need to talk.

> *Next time* . . .
> A man's voice says.

Gramps?

> *Next time,*
> the voice says again.
> It's not Gramps.
> *there **will** be gunshots.*
> *Three of them.*

Click.

Line goes dead.

Phone hums in my ear.
I drop the receiver.
It clunks on the floor.
I grab for the phone cord.
Try to yank it out.
The dial tone hums at my feet.
I grab the cord again.
Pull hard
I crumble onto the floor
next to the now-silent phone receiver.
Head in my shaking hands.
Oh, my God. Oh, my God. Oh, my God.

Is it a neighbor?
The guy at the grocery store?
A stranger?
A friend's parent?
Our preacher?
One of the cops?

Nobody and everybody
all at the same time.

I curl up in the chair.

Feet up under my butt.
Crunch my body down
into a tight heap.

I listen to rain
　　　　splatter on the roof,
　　　　and wind scrape branches against the house.
　　　　Words scrape against my brain—*next time . . .*
Watch lightning
　　　　flash through the windows,
　　　　and darkness creep back in.
　　　　A vision of shadows outside a window flash
　　　　through my mind.
Feel thunder
　　　　rock the house,
　　　　and pound in sync with my heart.

Kaboom! Kaboom! Kaboom!

How long will I live curled up in a chair?
How long will I stay frozen?
How long will I be afraid?

Kaboom! Kaboom! Kaboom!

When will I change?
When will I be something more than I am?
When?

Kaboom! Kaboom! Kaboom!

Tomorrow.
I'll change tomorrow.
As soon as the sun comes up.
I'll uncurl myself.
I'll unfreeze myself.
I'll unafraid myself.

Kaboom! Kaboom! Kaboom!

Tomorrow.

DAY 7
FRIDAY
AUGUST 21, 1987

1

I'll throw some things in a suitcase,

Momma says into the phone.
The boys need to get away from all this.
Face it, I need to get away from all this.
We'll be packed and ready in an hour.

Suitcase?
Packed and ready?

Momma's never run from anything.
She never gives up.
Stubborn as a mule,
that's what Dutch
said about her.

Last night's phone call
must have changed everything.
I never should have
told her about the call.
The threat.

It's not paint on the house,
or trash in the yard,
or annoying calls anymore.
It's not even the four
slashed tires on Momma's car—
thanks, Ashland's finest.

Someone threatened
to kill us.
To kill Momma's boys.

The words play over and over
in my head like a stuck record—
>   *Next time,*
>   *there **will** be gunshots.*
>   *Next time,*
>   *there **will** be gunshots.*
>   *Next time,*
>   *there **will** be gunshots.*
>   *Three of them.*
>   *Three of them.*
>   *Three of them.*

But are we really gonna run away?
Up and leave Ashland?
Now?
After a year of fighting?
After a year of graffiti and garbage?
After a year of Momma telling us things would get better?

After a year of not going to school, when we're finally
going back on Monday?

Now
      you're
            packing
                    a
                        suitcase,
                              Momma?

Now
      we're
          running
              away?
                    NOW?

Today was going to be
my day to change.
To unfreeze.
I promised myself
I would—
As soon as the sun came up.

But the sun didn't come up.
The sky's dark gray.
Rain's pouring.
And my momma's
packing to run away.

2

Yep. We're running away,

Momma says.
For the whole weekend.
She smiles.

I don't.

Mandy Kissinger shows up.
Momma called her.
We need a car with four tires.
Mandy's will do.

We're packed and ready.
>A cardboard box half-full of food.
>One Momma.
>Two suitcases.
>Three boys.

Loaded into Mandy's car.
Soaking wet from the rain.

Don't have to wait 'til Labor Day after all.

In the car, the wipers
swat at raindrops.
Trying to chase them away.

It's no use.
Before the wipers can
swipe back in place, more drops
splatter the window.

The hum of the motor,
the beat of the wipers,
the moan of the wheels
speeding through the wet
hypnotize me,
singing me almost to sleep.

The murmurs of Momma and
Mandy Kissinger mix
with the other sounds.

Each splat of raindrops,
each swish of wipers,
each whisper of conversation,
sweeps me further away.

I drift in and out—
my body relaxing
with each mile.

The rain washes us
toward
the
beach.

The safest perfect place we know.

3

The crunch of gravel wakes me.

It's a familiar sound.
It's the sound of almost home.

The crunching means we
left the interstate miles back,
got on a two-lane
black-top county road.

Now we've turned off
onto a narrow, gravel path
with grass
growing up
the middle.

I don't have to open my eyes
to see it.
I know it.
We're almost there.
Sandy Beach.

The scene appears behind my eyelids.
Pines tower on both sides,
hiding the view of the water.

Hiding the cabin
where Dutch
and Tiny
lived.
Where Momma
grew up.
Where we
want to grow up.

I inhale.
Lungs fill with salty, fishy air.
Exhale.
Home.
Even if it is just for a weekend.
We're home.

A weekend to relax.
A weekend to get ready for school.
A weekend to avoid Izzy,
                    or to talk to Izzy,
                                or to hide from Izzy.
A weekend to change things back to the way they were,
                    or let things be the way they are,
                                or let things become whatever
                                they'll become.

I inhale again.
Hold it.
Exhale.
Restlessness turns to restfulness.

4

Nothing but a broken down old cabin.

Broken down's probably a compliment.
But freedom's freedom,
        run down
        or not.

It's an hour from Ashland.
The shack Dutch and Tiny built.
Momma's parents.
Our Grandparents.

It leans.
        It leaks.
It lets bugs in.

But it's right on the beach,
        up
                on
                        stilts.

High tide sometimes licks at the
                        sand
                below
        it.

It's our place.
Our favorite place on earth.
Always the same.
Never changes.
I like that.
I need that.

5

They're gonna die!

Charlie hollers,
rushing through the ruin
toward the churning surf.

We're barely out
of the car
when he
spots
them.

Conch shells d   o   t
the beach as far
as we can s
            e
              e.

Charlie yells:
We gotta get 'em back in the water!
We've gotta save 'em.

The water is gray—
like the sky—
throwing angry
waves up against

the shore.
The gulf rakes
across its floor,
tossing out its
unwanted possessions.

> *Leave 'em be*
> Curtis says.
> *It's the life cycle.*

Charlie doesn't stop.
He grabs a shell,
hurls it into the water,
grabs another,
throws.

Running wildly
up and down the beach,
yanking up conch shells,
throwing them back home.

Help me!
Someone.
Help me!

His
hollers
turn
to
cries.

But
he
doesn't
stop
heaving
shells
into
the
water.

       Gently, Momma calls
       as she begins to help.

Mandy Kissinger helps, too.
Curtis joins in.
I watch.
Standing.
Staring.

They place the shells
back into the angry waves
under the dirty, gray sky.

A hand brushes mine.
Grabs hold.
A spark of electricity shoots
      from my fingers,
          up my arm,
              and all through me.

Second touch of the week.
The hand pulls me forward.

Izzy? I say.

Disobeying Gramps.
No surprise there.
Holding my hand.
Big surprise there.

Poet Boy, she replies,
not stopping.

We run side-by-side
to the shells
on the shore.
To Charlie.
To help.
Our hands clasped.
Tight.
Together.

She lets go.
Grabs a shell.
Places it
into
the
surf.

Finally, something
shakes me,
stirs me,
unfreezes me
and I pick up a
conch shell
and throw
it
as
hard
as
I
can.

Then another.
And another.
And another.

Gently, Momma says again.

Of course,
that something
that shakes me,
that stirs me,
that unfreezes me
is her.

Izzy.

We all work together
until the dots
on the beach
are gone.

I feel powerful.
Strong.

With my family.
With my friend.
Superheroes—side-by-side—
saving conchs for all mankind.

6

Gotta air out the place,

Momma says,

⬚⬚⬚⬚⬚⬚⬚⬚⬚⬚⬚⬚

drives off.

Momma cranks open
the windows,
filling the
room
with
the
smell
of
the
gulf.

Izzy's curled up
in Dutch's recliner.
Reading.

Curtis and I
haul the
suitcases
and the box
of food
up the two

flights of stairs.
As we reach
the landing,
Charlie races
out the screen
door chasing an
orphaned kitten
he found somewhere.

> Why'd we pack suitcases?
> Curtis mumbles.

Good question.
Half the stuff
we own is here.
Clothes, toothbrushes,
sheets, towels.
All of Dutch and Tiny's
things, too.

The cabin is
pretty much the way
they left it.

It feels like them.
It smells like them.
It looks like them.

Dark, faded wooden paneling
wraps around us like
Dutch's suntanned arms.

Faded flowered curtains flap
like one of Tiny's muumuus
has caught hold of the wind.

It feels like home.
It smells like home.
It looks like home.
It is home.

I wish we could live here.
Leave Ashland forever.
        You don't like change,
        one side of my mind reminds me.
But moving here wouldn't really be a change.
        Change is change.
        You can't change the rules about change,
        my mind whispers.

Maybe change isn't bad if it's what you want.
        And you always get what you want. Right?
        Now my brain is making fun of me.

I run my hands across the paneling.
Let the curtain flap against my arm.
Wonder what Dutch and Tiny would think
        about HIV . . .
        about school . . .
        about change . . .
        about me.

7

Rocks stand guard around the pit.

Momma looks
        out at the waves.
Curtis pokes
        at the last of the embers.
Charlie wraps a blanket
        tight around his shoulders.
        The kitten cuddled inside.
Izzy holds her hands out—
        warming them as the fire gasps for breath.

I throw in the last of the sticks—
still sticky with marshmallow goo—
and watch them s l o w l y begin to burn to
                                n o t h i n g n e s s.

Don't stay up too late,
Momma says, standing.
Walks across the sand.
Heads for home.
A trail of footprints follow her.

We stretch out on a blanket
beside the last of the crackling glow,
three brothers, their beach sister, and a cat.
The four humans stare into the night sky
like we've done a hundred times before.
The kitten is a mound of fur beside us.

The glow is gone.
Angry grays turned to black.
Constellations soar overhead.

We're quiet.
Still.
Listening to
gentle
waves.

I feel small beneath the sky.
It towers over me.
The stars stare down
from the dome of space.
The universe.
Immense.
Vast.
Me.
Small.
Tiny.
One speck on the earth.
Like a single grain of sand on the beach.

The stars, Charlie whispers, pointing,
are so small.
Tiny little lights.
I'm so much bigger
than a star.

Of course he's not.
He's tiny, too.
Like me.
Another grain of sand.

> *There's the Big Dipper,*
> Izzy says.
> Takes Charlie's hand,
> points his index finger
> at the sky.

> *And there,*
> she moves
> his hand,
> *the Little Dipper.*

> *And that,*
> she swirls his hand in the air,
> *is the Milky Way.*

> *Billions of stars.*
> *Light years away,*
> she says.

The glow took years
to reach us.
Right now, we're
staring into the past.

I look up again.
Change my point of view.
Not looking down from above,
and seeing how small I am,
but looking up at the stars,
into the dome
of outer space.

I instantly feel bigger
lying beside Izzy and my brothers
staring at the stars.

I changed.
And it didn't kill me.

Monday hangs over my head just like the stars.
School seems like a far-off planet.
A black hole in the Ashland galaxy.
I'm the lone astronaut floating towards it.
Sucked in by its gravitation pull.

Change your point of view,
some part of my brain tells me.

I look back up at the Milky Way.
If I can change how I look at the universe,
maybe I change how I look at school,
and at Ashland.
It won't change them.
It won't change anything probably.
Except maybe me.
It won't kill me to try.

I think.

Night fellas,

Izzy says.
Silently,
blond waves of hair
flood over her sweatshirt-covered shoulders.
She pushes her hair back,
like tide rushing out
from shore.

We know what's coming.
Izzy's famous parting line.

If I don't go home,
she says,
I can't come back.

    Tomorrow? Charlie asks.

Tomorrow, little man.
She rubs Charlie's
buzzed head.
Fingertips gently
run down the
kitten's spine.

    Izzy, I begin . . .

She places her hands on her hips.
Turns.
Looks at me.
Doesn't say anything.

Can we have a talk tomorrow?

Sure, she says.
I'll call you.
Promise.

She turns.
Walks away.

Her words are like a
slap across my face.
I feel the sting.
Inside.

Izzy trudges through the sand.
I stare at her back
as she disappears
into the dark.

She doesn't need to call,
Charlie says.
She can come down to the cabin anytime.

You're right, Charlie.
I reply.
I only wish it was that simple.

**Blood brothers, Charlie says. *From the movie.
Remember?***

I forgot all about that, I answer.

               Me, too, Curtis says.

Two summers ago.
Around a fire like this.
We nicked our fingers,
each pinching out a drop of blood.
It was before our blood was bad—I think.
Still, Momma would have been furious
about her bleeder boys making themselves bleed.

Holding our fingers together,
drops of blood mingling,
we shouted:

BLOOD BROTHERS!

Like in the movie.

What's it mean? Charlie asks.

He was real young then.
Didn't mean anything to him.

Not the movie.
Not the nicks on our fingers.
Not the words *blood brothers*.
But Charlie always did what *we* did,
whether he understood it or not.
Still does.

> *We're connected*, Curtis says.
> *We take care of each other.*

> *We're related*, I add.
> *From the same flesh and blood.*

Blood? Charlie whispers into the fire.

I think I know
what he's thinking.
Maybe Curtis does, too.

The sticks spit and hiss
in the coals.

> *We're connected*, Curtis says again.

> *In every way*, I add.

Let's name him B.B.,
Charlie says out of nowhere.

> *Who?*

The kitten, Charlie replies. *He's one of us now.*
One of the Blood Brothers.

All for one, and one for all, I call.

That's a different movie, Curtis replies.

There is no I in team?

Now you're trying too hard.

So is the kitten in?
Can he be a Blood Brother, too?

All for . . .

Shut up, Calvin, Curtis interrupts.
He's in, Charlie.
B.B.'s in.

DAY 8
SATURDAY
AUGUST 22, 1987

1

Go wake up Izzy,

Momma says,
flipping a
pancake
onto a plate.

Izzy?

Yep. She's sleeping in the hammock.

I stare out the screen door.
She's curled up in the hammock.
Arms inside her sweatshirt,
her knees pulled up and tucked under it.
Her hair a tangled mess.
A dark shadow in a still-dark morning.
Stop staring pervert, some part of my brain says.

The slam of the screen door
wakes her before I can.

Good mornin', fish eyes, I say.

> *Mornin'.*
> Her voice is even more
> gravelly than usual.
> She doesn't look at me.

How long you been here?

> *Since Gramps chewed me out*
> *for spending time with you guys.*
> *I said* screw it, *and walked.*

Breakfast, Momma calls.

You stood up to him for us?

> *I stood up to him for me,* she replies.
> She swings her tanned legs out of
> > the hammock.
> Uses her fingers to comb at her hair.

So you're not mad at me?
We're okay?

> *Screw you, too, Calvin.*
> Izzy's out of the hammock in a flash.
> Screen door slams again.

Word face slap #2,
    I say to the hammock.

The smell of maple syrup
wafts out the screen door.
I head in.
Feeling like fish guts.

Slam.

2

This is the best day ever!

Charlie shouts,
pulling off his goggles,
seaweed dangling from his arms.
He shakes salt water
from his hair,
and turns
to face
the gulf.

It
sends
another
wave—
white,
foamy,
growing
taller
as
it
heads
toward
him.

He
jumps,
and
lets
its
roar
pass
by.

Then
waits
for
another.

I dig trenches.
Preparing for another seaside attack.
Sweat dripping.
Arms straining.
Back aching.
I pull off my shades,
lift the bottom of my T-shirt,
wipe the sweat from my face.

Curtis gathers branches.
Shoves them into the sand.
Trench barricades.
Reinforcement.

Izzy rolled her eyes an hour ago.
How immature,
she tsked,
before
spreading
out a towel,
yanking off
her T-shirt
and shorts,
and laying down.
She reached up,
pulled her hair
into a knot.
Tanned skin in
a red bikini.
Sunbathing.
Nothing immature about that.

I can't keep my eyes off her.
Thank God for the shades.
And thank God the trench is deep
enough to hide me from the waist down.
I feel like a pervert again.
My brain doesn't even have to say it.
My best friend.
My beach sister.
The fish eyes to my fish guts.
And I can't keep my eyes off her.

B.B. has discovered chameleons.
Chases and nips if one dares
venture onto the towel
he's claimed as his.

Let's stay at the beach forever,
Charlie shouts.

Curtis and I cheer in response.
Izzy does, too.
Miss Mature—acting like one of the boys.

Hope she'll stay part of us.
Even if she's not one of the boys.
Hope she'll be my friend again.
Even if we're never fish eyes and fish guts again.

Undertow!

Izzy hollers,
pointing down the beach
at Charlie.

> **undertow**
> [**uhn**-der-toh]
> *Noun*
>
> 1. the seaward, subsurface flow of water
>   from waves breaking on a beach.
> 2. a strong current below the surface of a body
>   of water, moving in a different direction than
>   the surface current
>
> Syn: Riptide, Undercurrent
> See also: Eddy, Whirlpool

I spot him.
He tries to swim.
Struggles to walk.
But he's no match
for the current.
His body is pulled

away from us.
Down the beach.
Further away from shore.

Izzy and Curtis sprint
toward Charlie.
Curtis curses as he runs.

I stand.
Watch.
Mouth dry.
Throat tight.

Finally . . .
        I chase after them.

Curtis wades in—chest deep—
grabs Charlie from behind
under his arms.
Pulls.
Yanks.
Drags
him toward
shore.

Izzy's there, too.
I rush in
behind
them.

A wave hits me head on.
I feel a push against my legs,
down below the surface.
The undertow *is* strong.
Strong enough to pull someone
yards down the beach.
Strong enough to steal someone
and take them out to sea.

Izzy and I grab Charlie's feet, and
work with Curtis to haul
him
       from
               the
                    water.

He's exhausted.
Leans on Curtis.
Back heaves up and down with each breath.

      Where're my goggles?
      he chokes.

Gone.
Taken.
Like you almost were.

He gasps, pants.
Falls to the sand.

He's always been the best at dying.
Thank God, he didn't.

The best day ever,
is gone.
The water that we love,
turned against us.

Thirty minutes later,

Charlie's back in the water.
Splashing.
Snorkeling.
Swimming.

Like nothing ever happened.
Like the waves never tried to yank him away from us.
Like we never had to fight to pull him back.
To save him.
To keep him.

Everyone acts
like everything's
normal.

We're good at that.

Curtis sneaks up on gulls,
lurching at them,
watching them scatter,
and fly away.

Izzy and I toss
a Frisbee

back
and
forth.
Not
saying
a
word.

I fling my unspoken words
toward her.
She reaches out,
grabs the Frisbee.

Throws it back.
Wonder if she caught my words.
As my hand closes
around the plastic disk,
I wonder if I've caught hers.

If nothing else, this would
be the perfect time
for an analogy-a-thon.
We could toss gross friendship
comparisons back and forth
across the beach.

We don't.
We'd have to still be friends
for that.

Momma collects seashells.
Gifts for your teachers,
she says.

I'd forgotten about teachers.
About school.

I feel the undertow . . .
  pulling me toward Monday morning . . .
    ripping me away from home . . .
      washing me out to Ashland
        Elementary School.

But there's a secret to surviving undertows.
Dutch taught me and Curtis.
Didn't live long enough to teach Charlie.

Don't panic—
  Probably the hardest part of all.
Swim parallel to the shore—
  Undertows are narrow, you can swim out of them.
When you're out of the undertow—
  Get to shore ASAP.

There's my plan for Ashland Elementary School:
  1. Don't panic.
  2. Get out of it and get back home every day.
  3. Get to the shore, the cabin, the beach ASAP.

5

My shadow grows long, thin.

The sun slowly descends
until it reaches the waves—
touching for a moment
before beginning
its slow slide down
beneath the line
that separates
water from sky.
My shadow
disappears, too.
Dusk slips in.
Sunset's glow
turns to
dark,
black
night.

Saturday's slipping away.
We can't stop it
any more than
we could stop
an undertow.

6

Shadows are gone.

After much heat.
After the beach.
After dinner.
After sunset.
After B.B.'s second bowl of milk.
After four rounds of Yahtzee.

Momma's in Dutch and Tiny's room.
Door closed.
Her favorite U2 cassette on repeat.
Charlie's in there, too. And B.B.
Sleeping together on an air mattress.
Curtis is back in the spare room.

Izzy's in the recliner again.
Curled up again.
Reading again.

I roll Yahtzee dice.
Over and over.
I promise myself
if all five land
on six,

I'll talk
to
Izzy.
Tell
her
everything
she
wants
to
know.
Everything
I
need
to
say.

The plastic cubes
       tumble,
              clatter,
                           land.
Red dots showing.
22.
Roll again.
The die bounce.
Land.
17.
More rolls.
More clatter.
15.
11.
25.

I hope to get 30.
Hope not to get 30.
Rolling.
Rolling.
Faster.
Faster.
Throwing the dice
harder with each roll.

Something on your mind?
Izzy asks.

Roll again.
Clatter-clatter-clatter.
30.
No choice now.

      Maybe.

Maybe?
You didn't call me back.
You didn't answer my letter.
You've gawked at me all weekend,
but you've hardly said a word.

      You're right.
      Sorry.

My face burns red.

You should be.

She folds her arms over her chest.
Crosses her legs at the ankle.
Glares.

> *I wanted to tell you.*

She doesn't blink.

> *But I didn't want to tell you.*

Obviously.

> *I mean. I was afraid, Izzy.*
> *I am afraid.*

My mind
goes
blank.
So many words
in my brain.
I don't know
which to say.
Try to put
them in order.

> *Curtis and Charlie could die.*

Silence.

Her glare softens.

You could die, Calvin.

I roll again.
Clack-clack-clack.
Like the rolling cubes of plastic could change things.

      Yep.

Silence
surrounds
us.
Curtains
rustle
with
the
breeze.
Katydids
try
to
fill
up
the
quiet.

Of course, she says.
You could *live.*
But if you keep being

a dumb-ass, that's not
a great option.

A smile.
A twinkle.
The old Izzy.
For a second.

I chuckle.
Nod.

Roll the dice one last time.
Clack-clack-clack.
Ignore the cubes.
Walk to the sofa.
Stretch out.
Look down, past my T-shirt
and shorts,
across my bare legs,
over my feet
at Izzy.
She leans back as
                          far
              as the
        recliner
will let her.

          Whatcha reading?

<u>On My Honor.</u>

217

What's it about?

Two friends.
One dies.

Is it our life story?

Were alive, stupid.

I try to laugh at
my joke, but
something catches
in my throat.
My mouth opens.
Out of nowhere,
words fall out.
My guts dump
into the room.
Detail after detail
spilling,
spewing,
mixing with
the night air
blowing through
the curtains
and
katydids
chirps.

Transfusions.
First diagnosis—Curtis.
Second—me.
Third—Charlie.
Medical brochures.
News magazines.
Photos.

Izzy nods.
Listens.

Doctors.
Nurses.
Letter from school.
Letter from church.
Home school.
Graffiti.
Garbage.

She raises the recliner.
Pushes herself to the edge of the chair.

School Board Meeting.
Angry crowd.
Hateful signs.
CDC man.
Handshake.
PAAS.
Mr. Freeze.
More graffiti.
More garbage.

She moves from the recliner.
Sits on the floor.
Leans against the sofa.
Head on the cushion.
My hand hangs
above her shoulder.

Manila Flauinger.
Superhero underwear.
Food box.
Card. Cash.
Anonymous friends.
Prognosis.
Wagon Wheel Buffet.
Newspaper article.
Phone calls.
Shadows.
Officer Lopez.

She folds her arm up,
Fingers touch my hand.
Third touch in a week.

Something breaks inside me.

7

Sobs.

Uncontrollable.
Try to hold them in.
Try to silence them.

Izzy's up on her knees,
leaning forward,
wraps her arms
around me.

I can't move.
My arms—
stiff by my sides.

Her sweatshirt
presses against my
T-shirt-covered chest.
Some part of my brain yells—

Incoming.

A second part says—

It's Izzy.

I'm gonna die, Izzy.

Her hold on me
tightens.

She's still listening.
I can't see her face,
but I know.
She's
listening

And there's nothing
I can do about it.
I'm helpless, Izzy.
Helpless.

Her grip on me dissolves.
She lifts her face till it hovers above mine.

You may be dying,
But you're not helpless.

Of course I am.
What can I do
about any of this?

You've got to fight it, Calvin.
You've got to live.

I am living.
But I can't stop HIV.
Or AIDS.

Or the School Board.
I can't do anything
about anything.

Stop thinking that.
Stop thinking you can't do anything.

I choke in the middle of a sob.
Stare at her.

Calvin, since we were little
you've thought you couldn't
do anything about anything.
That's nothing new.

That's not true.

Like yesterday at the beach,
you waited until I grabbed your hand.
And today, you stood there
while we rushed to Charlie.

I came and helped.

Yeah, you did.
But you hesitated. You waited.
Why?

I didn't know what to do.

We didn't know what to do either,
but we knew we had to do something.
Not doing anything—it's like giving up.
You've gotta stop giving up, Calvin.

       That's not fair, Izzy.

Fair!
Nothing's fair, Calvin.

Her eyes squint.
Her head tilts a bit.
She rests her hands on
my chest and I can feel
her weight pressing down.

You know what's not fair?
Having both of your parents run off and leave you.
Having no place to live but with a grouchy old man.
Not having one single friend who lives less than an hour
away.
None of that's fair.
But it sure as hell doesn't make me helpless.

      I'm not like you, Izzy.

Who says you need to be like me?
Start helping yourself for a change.
That's all I'm saying.

BAM! BAM! BAM!

Izzy jumps.
My body bolts up.
A screech comes from
one of the bedrooms.

BAM! BAM! BAM!

Both bedroom doors thud open.
Curtis rushes in, a canoe paddle
raised above his head—ready to strike.
Momma's right behind him.

BAM! BAM! BAM!

The screen door sounds like
it's gonna come off its hinges.

> *They found us*, Charlie cries from
> the hall.

BAM! BAM! BAM!

> *Izabelle, get out here.*

> *Fred Lawrence?*
> Momma's voice growls
> through her clenched teeth.

She stomps to the door.
Throws it open.
Looks through the screen.
Gramps is almost invisible
behind the mesh.

You scared us to death

Tell her to get out here.

I'm not going anywhere.
Izzy's up. Feet planted wide.
Hands on her hips.

This is all your fault.
Gramps glares at Momma.
He yanks open the door.
Pushes his way in.

*It's bad enough you let this happen
to your boys.*
*You're not gonna destroy my
granddaughter, too.*
She's not gonna get your disease.

Fred, there's no danger.
Momma says.

He spins around.
How can you say that?

Did you think they were in danger?
He thrusts a hand out.
Points to us.
You had no idea the danger your boys
were in.
No idea at all.
And you don't have any idea about the
danger now either.

Momma has nothing to say.
We do know—my mind screams.
CDC man told us.
It's in the brochure.
There's no danger.

> *Let's go, Izabelle.*
> *Now.*

Izzy turns.
Faces me.

Calvin, say something.
Do something.

What does she think I can do?
What can I say?

Why would I expect you
to say or do anything?
What can you do?

Like she's reading my mind.

You won't even help yourself.
Why would I think you'd help me?

Izzy stomps out.
Gramps behind her.
Screen door slams.
Two sets of feet
pound down two
flights of steps.
The curtains flutter.
Waves crash out on the shore.

Curtis drops the paddle
on the floor with a thud.
Charlie yelps again.

I run to the screen door.
Shove it open.
Rush to the deck railing.
        I'm sorry, Izzy,
I call into the dark.
        I'm sorry.

Silence.
Katydids try to
fill

            up

                    the

                            quiet.

I sink into the hammock.
Stare up into the sky.
Millions of stars
shine
down.
I pull
myself
into
a
ball,
feeling
small
again.

Lawyer's coming over,

Momma tells us when we get back to Ashland.
Got a letter from
the School Board.

Another one?

Instructions for
your first day.

What's there to know?
We get up.
Get dressed.
Show up.
Do some work.
Come home.
Do homework.
Start over the next day.
Right?

Wrong.

The lawyer gives us
three pages
of rules.
What we can,
and cannot do.
Mostly cannot.

Momma sits us down and reads the list.

- No fighting.
- No biting.
- No spitting.
- No use of public restrooms.
- No eating in the cafeteria.

No lunch? Charlie gasps.

You'll take a sack lunch, Momma answers.

What if we need to pee? asks Curtis.

You'll go before school. Then you'll hold it.

There's more.

- The school will not be responsible for accidents or injuries.

- The school will not be responsible for cleaning up blood or bandaging injuries.
- The school reserves the right to send students home who are bleeding, or showing signs of illness such as coughing, sneezing, or fever.

It's not right
The words are mine.
They surprise me.

Here's the biggest thing,
Momma says.

- The students will be placed in the grade indicated on the last report card of their last year of attendance in Ashland Public Schools.

What's that supposed to mean?
Curtis snaps.

I know.
Just as well that Ashland
doesn't have a middle school,
cause I wouldn't be going.

*They're not gonna count
homeschool.
We're being held back.*

We won't be with our friends?
Charlie asks.
Eyes wide.

We ain't got friends,
Curtis replies.

It is what it is, Momma says.
They can do whatever they want.
Fair or not.
And we'll do
what we
have to do
to make sure
you boys get the
education you
deserve.

All we're getting is screwed.

I'm surprised that the words
found their way from my
brain to my mouth.
But it feels good
to let what's bouncing
around inside me,
escape
into the
world.
For
once.

2

And now the biggest hit of 1987—
Walk Like an Egyptian.

Momma's baking.
Radio blasting.
The smell of butter,
                brown sugar,
                        and chocolate
mixes with music.

                                Floats
                        through
                the
        house.

Soon as he hears
the song, Charlie's
in the kitchen.
He and Momma dance
shoulder-to-shoulder—
like in the
music video.

Get in here, boys,
Momma calls.

Not again,
Curtis moans.

But the smell of
chocolate seems to
suck us in.

Dance! Momma
hollers over the music.

       Momma, please, Curtis complains.

She's not hearing
any of it.
She calls
out instructions
over the music:

Raise your arms above your head.
Bend your wrists, palms down.
Like cobras ready to strike.
That's it, boys!

      How long is this song?

No matter how long or short it is,
it's gonna be too long for Curtis and me.

Hush up, and dance.
Turn your palms the other way.

And rock your heads back and forth.
Small steps now. Strut it!

We're laughing
even though we don't want to.
Each trying to outdo the other.
The heat of the oven turning our
kitchen into Ashland, Egypt.

If anyone's outside painting graffiti tonight,
they'll have a lot of new words to spray
on the Johnston family's walls.

3

Get out of those cookies,

Momma yells
I've already snatched a plateful.
Carry them to the bedroom.
Charlie's called a meeting.

Curtis grabs three cookies
as soon as I'm in the door.

Knock. Knock. Knock.
Charlie raps his knuckles on the
headboard of his bunk.

This meeting of the
Blood Brothers is called to order.
When I call your name, please
say, "Here," Charlie tells us.

>*Are you serious?* Curtis mumbles
>through a mouthful of
>chocolate chip cookies.

Calvin Johnston.

Here.

Curtis Johnston.

Curtis plops down on
a pile of pillows.
Shoves another
cookie in his mouth.

Curtis Johnston.

    Here. Of course.

Charlie Johnston.
Here.

    B.B. Johnston, Curtis calls.
    Meow.

Charlie throws him
a dirty look.

Please stand for the pledge.

    You've got to be kidding me.

Charlie and I stand.
Lightbulb dangles above our heads.
We each put a hand over our heart.
I pledge allegiance . . .

Curtis huffs.
Shrugs.
Stands.
Joins in.
. . . *indivisible, with liberty and justice for all.*

The new business for our meeting:
What if school sucks?

>   *Finally, a good topic.*
>   *And you owe a quarter*
>   *to the Cuss Jar.*

Charlie's serious.

>   *It won't be bad,* I lie.

Charlie looks me in the eye.

What if it is?

>   *What can we do?*
>   *We can't change anything about school.*
>   Izzy's words flash in my brain—Stop
>   thinking you can't do anything.
>   *We'll think of something,* I add.

>   *Let's make a pact,* Curtis says.

A what?

An agreement. A promise.

Promise what?

> *After tomorrow, if any one*
> *of us wants to quit school,*
> *we'll stick together.*

All for one? I joke.

Curtis shakes his head.

We'll quit?
Just like that?

> *We'll vote on it.*
> *Then we'll quit.*

I like that.
We'll vote on it.

> *Works for me.*

Blood Brothers, Charlie says.

> *Blood Brothers,* Curtis repeats.

> I say it, too. *Blood Brothers.*

All in favor, say, "Aye."
Aye.

       Aye.

             Aye.

The Blood Brother Pact passes.

       Hand me the cookies, Curtis orders.

4

When everyone's in bed, I sneak back into the kitchen.

Not for a cookie.
For the phone.
To call Izzy.
The fourth try
since
getting
back
to
Ashland.
Three times and
     no
          one's
               answered.

She's never gonna talk to me again, part of me says.
She and Gramps have probably been out all day, the
other part says.

I dial the number.
     A worried knot squeezes
     in my stomach.

Sit down on the floor.
        I can hear my breathing
        through the receiver.
        Even my breath sounds nervous.
Press my back against the wall.
        Silently count the rings.
                One.
                Two
                Three.
                Four.

Then . . .

        Hello?

I suck in air and
push the words out.
Izzy, it's me. Calvin.

        Click.

DAY 10
MONDAY
AUGUST 24, 1987

1

Beep. Beep. Beep. Beep.

I slap the alarm.
Don't know how long
it's been beeping.
Crack one eye open.
Look over.
Watch the clock
flip to
6:31.

Not been up this early since—
since the last time I got up for school.
Sun's barely shining through the sheet curtain.
Curtis and Charlie are sound asleep.

Momma's in the kitchen.
She's humming.
Sizzling accompanies her.
Warm smell of bacon

crawls up the hall.
I follow it.

School clothes,
with price tags attached,
spread out on the sofa.
Three backpacks
with the supplies
we crammed in them
last night sit there, too.

On the table,
three brown bags.
Tops rolled down.
Name printed on each—
   Calvin
   Curtis
   Charlie
Beside them,
three plastic bags
stuffed with cookies,
shells hanging
from strings tied
around the top of each.

In the kitchen,
Momma's got
toast, bacon,
eggs, juice.
A feast.

Mornin', Momma.

Good morning, Son.
Sleep well?

Okay, I guess.
Tossed and turned.
You must have gotten up early.

Gotta get my boys
ready for school.
Have some breakfast.

How did you
sleep, Momma?

Unplugged the phone
around midnight.
I slept like a baby.

The dark circles
under her eyes
tell me that's
not true.

I eat.
Wake up Charlie and Curtis.
Shower.
Dress.

An ache in
my stomach.
The same I
always feel
before going
to school.
Been that
way since
kindergarten.
The first day,
the day after vacation,
Mondays after the weekend,
and my
stomach
tightens,
squeezes,
aches,
complains.

This is another first day.
Another day back.
But everyone knows this
first day is different than the others.
Worse than all of them combined.
Even more
       for my stomach
           to ache and complain about.

On my third trip to the bathroom, I make a pact.
A pact with myself.
A pact with my stomach.
It would be a pact with Izzy if she would talk to me.

> Today I will not think I can't do anything.
> Today I will do whatever I need to do

Then I'll get back home as fast as I can.

2

Gotta pee one more time,

Charlie hollers
from down the hall.

> *Not a bad idea,*
> Curtis says

I'm gonna walk with you boys.

> *You don't need to do that, Momma,*
> I say.
> But I'm glad she is.

Watch out for your brothers today, Calvin.
I'm counting on you.

Momma counting
on the thinker.
That's a new one.
I start to say it,
but I feel so
good about

what she
said that I
don't
wanna
spoil
it.

Two flushes later,
we've got our
backpacks, lunches,
bags of cookies.
Charlie gives
B.B. one last hug.

Don't forget,
Momma says,
*The cookies are
for your teachers.*

Knock. Knock. Knock.

Not today, Momma moans.
She's expecting the worst.
Who wouldn't?

Well, good morning, Officer Lopez.

Good morning, Mrs. Johnston.

Is there a problem?

Nope. Wanted to give the boys a lift to school.

Oh, that's not necessary.

Let me, ma'am. Please.

Something about his voice
changes Momma's
mind.
All right then.
Get a move on, boys.
Our ride's here.

We haul ourselves and our stuff
through the dew-covered grass,
out to the patrol car.
Momma climbs in the front.
The three of us in back.

C-o-o-l.
Charlie draws the word out long, slow.
Like we're being arrested.

That's not cool,
Momma says.

Riding in a cop car is.
Curtis immediately corrects himself.
I mean police car.

Can you turn on the siren?
Charlie asks.

Maybe another time,
Momma replies before Lopez can.

I look out the window.
The neighborhood's quiet.
No cars.
No kids walking.
No older ones waiting for the bus.
Everything's still.
Calm.
Never would know it's
the first day back to school

When we turn the corner
to Ashland Elementary,
I know why.
Everyone's already at school.

And.It's.Not.Calm.

3

Everyone's here to welcome us!

Charlie hoots,
They're glad we're back!
Sits up on the edge
of the backseat
so he can get a
better look at
the crowd.

Then he sees the signs.

Must be all the ones
from the high school gym
plus a hundred more.
The people holding
them have
twisted faces
pinched into
scowls.
Mouths open
with shouts.
Fists wave in the air.
Middle fingers do, too.

I think of every cuss word
I've ever heard Izzy say,
and repeat them all
in my head.
It's still not enough
cussing for this situation.

Vans with satellite
dishes fill the streets.
Large letters across
the side of each one.
A few men in the
crowd carry cameras.
Reporters stick microphones
in the faces of protestors.

When the patrol car
turns into the school's
parking lot, all the signs,
shouts, scowls, fists, middle fingers,
cameras, and microphones
turn toward us.

Pressing in.

> *Oh, no,* Momma moans.
> > *Damn them,* Curtis whispers.

A paper cup hurls
toward the car.

SPLAT.
I jump.
Black liquid
washes across
the window
beside me.
Someone leans in—
close to the car—
and
spits.
Right on the window
by Curtis.

Officer Lopez creeps the car
closer to the entrance,
the crowd parts—a little.
The muffled voices grow louder,

                louder,

                    louder.

     What are we gonna do? Momma asks.

I start to say, What can we do?
Then a part of my brain reminds me
of the pact I made with myself.
     Today I will not think I can't do anything.
     Today I will do whatever I need to do.
What a stupid time to make a pact with yourself,
the other side of my brain says.

I'll take you in,
Lopez tells us.
He parks
at the curb.
Officer needs back up,
Lopez shouts into his radio.
Ashland Elementary.
Repeat. Officer needs backup,
Opens his door.
Volume increases.
Slam.
Volume muffled.
He opens Momma's door.
Volume increases.
And the door behind her.
Volume swells.

Go home!
Carriers!
Get 'em!

Momma climbs out of the car.
We slide out
one after the other
right behind her.
Lopez spreads his arms like giant wings.
Stay together, he orders.
Momma grabs Charlie's hand.
I push Curtis in front of me.
I follow, arms wrapped around

his shoulders and hands on Momma's shoulders.

> *Momma*, I yell. *Put Charlie between you*
> *and Curtis.*
> She shoves Charlie behind,
> sandwiched in between them.

No! No! No! Our kids won't go!
Stay away!
AIDS kills!

Men's voices.
Women's, too.
Kids join in with their parents.
In my brain,
I hear quarters
clink

     clink

          clinking
into the Cuss Jar.

Officer Lopez keeps his arms spread
herding us toward the door.
The crowd makes
a path.
Sort of.
Familiar faces in the crowd.
The man from Pick-and-Pay.
A school board member.
Folks from church.
Neighbors.

Hands reach in.
Shove.
Pull.
Yank.
Keep moving, Lopez shouts.
Charlie screams.
Curtis tightens his hold on him.
Fists fly in.
Umph! Curtis grunts
as one lands squarely
on his shoulder.
I use my elbows to push
through the crowd, never
letting go of Momma's shoulders.

Stand back! Lopez orders.
More curses.
The narrow path
narrows even more.
Something flies
over our heads—
straight toward Momma.
I sling my backpack up.
A bottle ricochets off.
Glass shatters on the
side of Lopez' head.
He continues moving us
forward, arms wide.
Blood oozes.

Spreads.
Over his forehead.
Down his cheek.
Drips. Gushes.
A red flood down his face.
Faster! he yells,
pushing toward the door.

BLOOD!
They're infecting us!
Murderers!

We push through the
double glass door.
More parents and
kids inside.
Teachers, too.
Shouting.
Screaming.
Rev. and Mrs. Walker
are there, arms folded,
squinting in anger.
Daniel stands with them.

Lopez hustles us
toward the office.
Mandy Kissinger's
in the hall, snapping
her camera.

I see tears
on her face.
Lopez pushes us
into the office.
We're breathless.
Shaking.
Terrified.

Lopez shouts at the secretary,
Lock this door.
Lock it now!

This is Lopez. Third call for backup,

he barks into his radio.
No answer.
Again.
No one's coming,
he whispers to Momma.

He presses a wad of
paper towels against his forehead.
His fourth handful of paper towels.
The others, soaked with blood,
sit in the bottom of the trash can.
The bleeding has stopped—
almost.

> *Why did you come?*
> Momma asks.

I know what it's like . . .
I'm the only Hispanic on the force.

I take that in.
Think about it.
Most people in Ashland
aren't too nice to Hispanics.
Me included.
Call them names so bad
most kids wouldn't say
them in front of their mommas.
Me included.
Now Officer Lopez is helping us.
No questions asked.

. . . my wife and kids know what it's like, too . . .

People in Ashland aren't very nice
to Black people either.
Me included.
Have called them things
worse than the ones
Hispanic kids are called,
things that are worse than cuss words.
Me included.
People around here have done worse
than calling them names, too.
Things much worse.
Things I've heard about.
Things I've seen.

My brain whirls to a stop.
Am I like everyone else in
this town?
Just like the people who hate us?

The thought makes me shake my head.
Like I've been punched,
and I'm seeing stars.
That can't be true—I think.
That *is* true—I feel.

We hate anyone who's different.
I stop myself.
Rethink the sentence.
My brain tries it again.
I've always hated anyone who's different.
Treated them like they don't belong.
Pushed them out.

We all know what it's like
when people don't want you.
When they'll do anything
to keep you out.

I'm sorry Officer Lopez.
Sorry for everything.
For Ashland.
For me.
And I mean it.
Even though I don't say it.

I'm editing my pact:
> Today I will not think I can't
> > do anything.
> Today I will do whatever I need
> > to do.
> Today I will start treating people
> > the way I want to be
> > treated.

5

It's like we're the newest exhibit at a zoo.

People walk by the office.
Gawk through the window.
Some stand and stare.
I halfway expect them
to tap on the glass.

Half of me wants to slide
under the chair and disappear.
The other half of me
wants to flip them off.
At least that would be doing something.
But I don't think it's what I need to do.
And sure wouldn't be treating people
the way I want to be treated.

My pact is already a pain.

Other people focus straight ahead—
angry looks on their faces.
Now and then someone does
exactly what I thought about doing—

flip us off.

I try not to watch them.
My finger itching to respond.
Would only make them angrier.
Though I don't really care.

There are also the spitters.
Like outside.
Leaning back.
Gathering up a big load in their mouths
Spitting hard—
They jerk their bodies toward the window
            to make it
                    f   l   y.
I can't hear the splat,
but each time it feels like
the spit lands right in my face.
Gravity pulls the slimy drool
down the window in streaks.
I almost feel it sliding to my chin
and dripping down my neck.
Humiliation.
Disrespect.
That's what they want me to feel.
And they're succeeding.

Charlie's on the floor
drawing cats in a
spiral notebook
with his new,
back-to-school crayons.

Curtis leans back,
neck resting on the
top of the chair,
legs stuck out in
front of him.

Officer Lopez comes and goes.
The secretary
disappeared from sight.
Momma watches everything.

Where's that principal?
she asks.
> *Avoiding us.*
> Curtis replies,
> not lifting his head.

Mandy Kissinger
comes into the office.
whispers questions
to Momma, writes
down answers,
snaps pictures
of Charlie and
Curtis.
Maybe
of me.

> *Tell me this isn't another AP story,* I say.

I'm trying to document
everything that's going on,
she answers.
Trying to tell your story.

Or you're trying to get famous off of us.

Calm, Momma snaps.
Sorry, Mandy.
We're all on edge.
Mandy nods.
Hugs Momma.
Leaves.

There's enough mudslinging in this town,
Momma says to me,
without you joining in.

Sorry Momma.

You should be.

By 9:30 the hallway is empty.
I hear the secretary
on the phone
in the next room
making call after call.
She says nearly the same thing each time.

Yes, one of them is in your son's classroom.
     or
One of them has been assigned to your daughter's class.

Never says any of our names.
Like we don't deserve names.
Them is enough to say everything she needs
to say.

By 10:00, there's another parade
of parents and students.
This time,
they're
walking
out
of
Ashland
Elementary
School.

There go our classmates, I say.

Good riddance, Curtis replies.

We eat our lunches in the office.

Momma forgot to pack drinks.
We can't go to the cafeteria.
We can't drink out of the water fountain.
Peanut butter and jelly sticks
to the roof of my mouth
and clogs up my throat.
Reminds me of the
choking feeling
of the protestors
pushing in
around us.

There's a rattling at the office door.
Officer Lopez jumps to his feet.
The door swings open
It's the principal with a fistful of keys.

Officer, he says to Lopez.
Ma'am, he says to Momma.
The voice sounds polite.
His eyes never look at us.

Mr. Beason, Momma replies,
just as polite.

Charlie will be with Mrs. McKnight in 1st grade, he
announces.

First grade? Charlie moans.

We've already talked about this,
Momma says.
And the others?

Curtis will be in third grade with Miss Warden.

Great, a prison guard, Curtis moans.

Hush, Momma hisses. *Miss Warden? Is she new?*

Yes, the principal replies.

Calvin has been assigned to Mr. Nichols, our new fifth
grade teacher.
I'll be right back to escort you to your classes.
And he is out the door.

Putting us with new teachers,
Curtis says.
No one else will take us.

*Mrs. McKnight is definitely
not new,* I say.

Too old to complain, Curtis replies.

They're teachers, Momma says.
*That's all that matters.
Get your things.
Let's get you all to class.*

I can't do anything about who my teacher is.
I'm fine with a new teacher any way.
I can't do anything about who's in my class,
Or if they walked out in the middle of the day.
Momma says we're here to learn.
I can do that.
No
matter
what.

One side of my brain says:
   Mr. Nichols, get ready for Calvin Johnston.
The other side of my brain answers:
   Give me a break.

7

We drop off Charlie first.

Principal Beason, Momma, and Charlie walk in.
Curtis and I watch from the door.
Six or eight kids are busy cutting and pasting.
They don't seem to notice Charlie.
Mrs. McKnight slowly stands up.
Hobbles to the door from her desk.

This is Charlie **Johnston.**
Principal Beason makes sure to
emphasize the last name,
as if Mrs. McKnight might
not be able to figure out
that Charlie's one of *those* kids.

> *Come in, Charles,* she says.

>> *It's Charlie. These are for you.*
>> He holds out the cookies.
>> *I have a new cat.*

> *That's nice,* she says.
> Her hands fold together against her chest.
> *Put those on my desk, please, Charles.*

She nods at Momma.
Turns.
Hobbles away.

Charlie lays the bag of cookies
on Mrs. McKnight's desk.
Looks at the other kids
then at Momma.

She smiles.
He smiles back.
He walks to the closest table.
But not before he pushes his backpack
in front of his body,
like it's Captain America's shield and
he's ready to ward off any attack.
Or like a turtle who hides
inside his shell at the
first sign of danger.

Curtis is next.
We walk by the Media Center.
Cross over to the main building.
A line of kids coming back
from lunch pass in the
opposite direction.
They're young.
Maybe Charlie's age.
Two of the boys glare
as they pass by.

The last in line
shoots double birds.
No one else notices.
It doesn't make me mad
like in the office.
It actually seems
funny. Like a
finger in the
air is supposed
to hurt me in
some way.
I tighten
my lips
together
to stop
my smile.
It doesn't
work.

Principal Beason pushes open
the doors leading to
the third grade wing.
Leads us down the hall.
Stops. Opens a door.

Kids screech chairs
together in a ragged circle.
There are only about
ten of them.
They look little.

Curtis is a head taller
than all of them.

A woman scurries to the door.
Wrings her hands.
Miss Warden seems nervous.
Real nervous.
Maybe it's new-teacher nerves.
Or the-principal's-in-my-room nerves.
Or the kid-with-HIV-has-arrived nerves.

Before the principal can say anything,
Curtis does it for him.
I'm Curtis **Johnston.**
He emphasizes the last name,
like Beason did.

> *Welcome, Curtis. Come in. Take a seat,*
> the nervous teacher says,
> twisting her hands together.

Curtis shuffles into the room.
New tennis shoes squeak on the tile.
Pulls a chair behind the circle.
Drops into it.
Backpack plops beside him.
He scoots down in the chair.
Pushes his legs out in front of him.
Scowls a don't-mess-with-me look.

Folds his arms.
He's ready for a fight.
Nothing's changed there.

Feels weird walking through the school with
      the principal.
Even weirder walking through the school with the
      principal *and* Momma.

Wondering what I'll do when I walk into Mr. Nichols class.
Charlie tried his usual flight approach,
hiding behind his backpack.
Curtis was back to being the fighter.
Even if he didn't punch anybody.
Don't know that either will work.
Flight or fight.
But it's what they do.

      So what do you do, Calvin?
For once my brain is asking a question
instead of giving me an opinion.
Of course, *freeze* is the answer.
      How's that working out for you, Calvin?
That can't be a secret to anyone.
Not even my own brain.
Not well is the answer.

My brain doesn't say anything else.
It made its point, I guess.

I hear music coming from somewhere.
I recognize the song.
Momma nudges me. Smiles.
I roll my eyes.

We find the room with the music.
Sign on the door *Hay Nichols, 5th Grade.*
Principal Beason opens the door.
Music pours out.
The handful of kids in the room are dancing.
Except for Daniel Walker.
He's just standing there.
There's another kid I recognize.
Another baseball jock I think.
Don't remember his name.
No other familiar faces.
Just as well.
Don't have any friends left in Ashland anyway.
Except those anonymous ones.

A man—young, longish hair, moustache—
waves from across the room.
Comes in our direction.
Doesn't look like an Ashland Elementary teacher.
First, he's a man.
Second, he's wearing jeans, and a shirt and tie,
and then there's the hair and moustache.

You must be Calvin, he says.
Reaches out his hand.

Definitely not an Ashland Elementary teacher.
His grip is firm. He looks me in the eye.
We've been expecting you.
He says it like it's a good thing.
Ms. Johnston, he says turning to Momma,
I'm Roy Nichols. Glad to have Calvin in my class.
Momma's smile is about to bust her face.

He's still gripping my hand.
Shakes my arm up and down.
I shake back.
Make sure my grip
is strong, too.

> *Are you teaching today, Mr. Nichols?*
> Principal Beason asks over the music.

Definitely, Mr. Nichols answers.
The handshake stops as he looks at the principal.
As soon as we get acquainted
and finish introductions.

> *Good. Good,* Beason replies.
> *I hope that will be sooner than later.*

Momma turns to leave.
Looks back.
Waves . . .
at Mr. Nichols.
Mr. Nichols waves back.

I shake my head.
My mom is such a dork.
I wave, too,
          to say, *Hey remember me?*
She blows me a kiss.
Oh, God, Momma.
You don't blow kisses
in fifth grade.

Momma and Beason
disappear through the door.

Come on in, Calvin.

I walk toward the line of
dancing fifth graders.
Mr. Nichols joins in.
Music blares.
I close my eyes.
Shake my head a bit.
Smile.
Of course, Momma would like *this* song.

Do you know it? Mr. Nichols calls.
It's Walk Like an Egyptian.

Yeah. I've heard of it, I reply, lifting
my hands up like cobra heads,
and shuffling my feet.

Mr. Nichols is into poetry.

Tells us about Langston Hughes.
A Black poet.
How he was the
voice of his people.
A voice for people
      who didn't have a voice.

Gives us copies of
a poem—something
      about America.

Mr. Nichols sinks into a bean bag,
the rest of us spread out
on the carpet,
he says the poem—
        all of it—
from memory.
He doesn't read it.
He *performs* it.

His voice is a rollercoaster.
Loud. Then quiet.
Emotions building up,
sweeping down.
The words curve
and spin around
me, pulling me
forward.

Finished, he sits.
Silent.
Like he's waiting.
But I don't know for what.

I can really relate to Hughes, one kid says.
But what's with all the parentheses?

       Good question, Marcus. Mr. Nichols replies.
       He doesn't give an answer.

I hadn't looked at the poem.
Just listened.
Felt it.

I glance down at the paper.
See what the kid means.
Parentheses.
Scattered throughout the poem.
Like cupped hands holding words inside.

Those are his real feelings.
The words come out of my mouth.

Tell me more, Mr. Nichols says.

My face feels flushed—
like I'd thought of
Izzy's boobs or something.
All eyes are on me.
But for the first time today
they aren't glaring mad.
Most of them.

        I think . . . those words . . .
             . . . the ones in parentheses . . .
        tell what he . . . the poet . . . thinks. Feels.
        The other words . . .
             . . . they're what everyone else wants to
        hear.

The things he can't say out loud,
the guy who asked the question says.

A couple of kids nod.

        That's stupid. Why not say what
            you're thinkin'?
        It's Daniel Walker.

He's not asking me.
He's not really asking at all—
even if it is a question.

Mr. Nichols sits up straighter.
Doesn't speak.

Finally a girl with long brown hair speaks up.
Some people don't want to know
what you think or feel.
You gotta keep those things in.
Quiet. Hidden. Secreto.

Thanks, Sofia, Mr. Nichols says.
Things get quiet again.
Here's an idea,
Why don't you all write some poems
 tonight?
Groans from almost everyone.
Not me.
Mr. Nichols keeps going.
Write what you think people want
 to hear.
Then in parentheses, write what you
 really think and feel.

I was thinking
that nothing
about
Mr. Nichols
or
this class
felt like
Ashland
Elementary
School.
(And
that
was
a
very
good
thing.)

9

She threw them in the trash.

Charlie says
as we walk toward the house.

Officer Lopez picked
us up at school.
Brought us home.
Said he'd see us
in the morning.

We'd been quiet
in the patrol car.
I had a goofy grin
on my face the entire time.
Couldn't stop thinking about my day.

As soon as we
are out, Charlie
can't hold it in
                    any longer.

> *Threw what in the trash?*
> Curtis asks.

The cookies.
She thought I didn't see.
But I did. She threw away
the whole bag. Even the shells.
Then washed her hands. Scrubbed 'em.
Like that bag was dirty or something.

(Mr. Nichols would never do that.)

> *I had a lousy day, too,*
> Curtis says.

(Am I the only one with a good teacher?)

Charlie's on to a new subject.
Gotta pee.
He runs in the door.

> *What happened?*
> I ask Curtis.

(Hoping it's not too bad.)

> *Miss Warden is not*
> *a prison guard.*
> *She can't make anyone do anything.*
> *Two guys pinned my arms behind me and*
> *dared me to fight.*

> *You didn't. Right?*

(Don't get us kicked out, Curtis.)

Of course not.
Besides, my arms were pinned.

Is that it?

Nope.
A girl told me she could get AIDS
from breathing the same air as me.
Another said I was a sinner going to hell.
Kids threw erasers and spitballs at me all day.
Got tripped a couple of times.
Nobody talked to me.
Like I said, a lousy day.

(Guilt wipes the smile off my face.)

Momma greets us at the door.
Go grab a snack.
Then get going on your homework.

She doesn't ask about school.
Probably doesn't need to.
Probably already has a
pretty good idea that
it was a lousy day
for everyone.
(Except me.)

Later, when Momma finds me
writing at the kitchen
table, she asks,
How was it, Calvin?
Fine. (The best day of school ever.)
Mr. Nichols seems nice.
He's okay. (He's incredible. Smart.
I like him.)
You gonna fit in alright?
Sure. (I think Mr. Nichols will make sure
I do—that we all do.)
What are you working on?
Homework. (A poem. My teacher's into
poetry, like me.)
Glad it went well.
Thanks. (Better than well. Great.
Fantastic. Tremendous.)

10

This meeting is called to order.

It's Charlie's latest
meeting of the
Blood Brothers.
100% attendance,
including B.B.

> I'm writing my fifth poem
> since getting home.
> (I need to tell Izzy.)
> I want to have something
> good for Mr. Nichols.
> (Izzy would love him.)
> I want to write my
> best poem ever.
> I'm only halfway listening.

I've got new business,
Charlie says.

> *What about attendance?*
> *And the pledge?*
> Curtis laughs.

What's a synonym for anticipation?
I wonder.

Alright, alright, Charlie groans.
He takes attendance.
Leads us in the pledge.
Then . . .

Now for the new business.

> *Aren't we supposed to approve*
> *the minutes or something?*
> Curtis tries to get Charlie off track again.

> I make a list of the synonyms:
>> hope
>> joy
>> prospect
>> expectancy

Shut up, Charlie tells Curtis.
And we don't have minutes.
Charlie is not gonna let
anyone get him off track.
I make a motion—
That we never go back to school again.

> *Second,* Curtis calls.

All in favor? Aye.

Aye.

I snap out of it.
Look up from my writing.
What are we voting on?

Motion passes
Charlie says.
No
more
school.

What?

.

Majority wins.
Curtis says.
No more school.

No more school?
What's a synonym for disappointment,
my brain wonders.

Of course we're going back to school,
I say.

Nope, Charlie says.
Folds his arms.
We said last night
we'd vote on it.

And we just voted,
Curtis adds,
not to go back to school.

        But . . .

Praise the Lord!
Charlie shouts like
he's attending prayer meeting
at Open Door Fellowship.

        Hallelujah!
        Curtis whoops.

        Oh, God . . .
        I moan.

A poem for Mr. Nichols.

LANGSTON

I am no Langston Hughes.
Not a published poet, writer, playwright.
No one's seen my words.
(No one ever will.)
I'm not the voice for anyone.
(Not even the voice for me.)
I could never be the voice for
those who feel they have no voice.
(There is no voice inside of me, and
who would hear it if there were?)
I am no Langston Hughes.
(But I truly wish I were.)

By Calvin Johnston
8/24/87

DAY 11
TUESDAY
AUGUST 25, 1987

1

Boys, get up and get dressed,

Momma hollers
before the alarm goes off.
Switches on the lightbulb.

>*We're not going,*
>Charlie answers.
>Pushes a cat butt
>off his pillow.
>Yawns.
>*We voted on it.*

Didn't you hear?
Momma asks.
Half serious.
Half joking.
I vetoed that.
Officer Lopez will be here
in twenty minutes.
Get to it.

Curtis curses under his breath.

Can she do that? Charlie moans,
sliding out of his bunk.

Thank God, I whisper.

What, Calvin? Charlie asks.

I said, "Oh, God," I lie.

I'm already dressed.
Did it in the dark.
Backpack's packed.
I run my hand
over the spot
where I
envision
my poems
sit inside
the backpack.
Today, someone
may see—
or hear—
my writing
for the
first time.
My stomach is
like a jar of bees.

In fact, my whole
body is buzzing.
Right foot is up
on my toes,
leg bouncing.
Trying hard to keep
the excitement—
the energy—
inside.

Newspaper's on the table in the kitchen.
Picture of us crammed in the principal's office.
Another Mandy Kissinger AP story.
She's getting more famous by the day.
(We're becoming more infamous.)
Cereal and milk on the table, too.

> *Where's the bacon and eggs?*
> Curtis asks.

In the fridge, Momma answers.
No time today.
Mandy's picking me up.
I've got a job interview.
Can you believe it?
A job interview.

> *What about us?*

What about you?

What if we need you?

Charlie, if I get the job,
the school will
have the number.
You'll go to school.
I'll go to work
Like normal people.

Us? Normal?
I don't think so,
Curtis mumbles.

Even Momma
laughs.

Outside, TV
crews hold
cameras and
microphones.
Push toward us.
Shout questions.

Officer Lopez gets us to the car.
Drives us to school.
Talks to us about his wife,

                        their daughter.

She's in your class,
he says to me.

My daughter.
Name's Sofia.

Passes a photo back.
The girl with long, brown hair.

> *Oh, yeah. I know her.*
> Pass the picture back.

She thinks Mr. Nichols is pretty great.

> *Yep. Me, too.*

From the corner of my eye
I see Curtis' and Charlie's heads spin.
Eyes staring.
Curtis plops back against the seat.
Folds his arms.
> *Hmmmph.*

> > *I bet <u>he</u> ate the cookies,*
> > Charlie adds.

I'm a Blood Brother traitor
riding in the back of a squad car.

There are signs at school.
And cameras.
And microphones.
Protestors, too.

Fewer.
But still loud.
Still angry.
Still nasty.

Officer Lopez parks and walks us in.
Walks us to class
Stops to introduce himself to Mr. Nichols.
Hugs Sofia.

There are a few more kids today.
And a different feeling in the air.

Some of the new kids
stare when I walk in.
Two of them whisper.

Hey, Calvin,
Mr. Nichols calls
from across the room.
I need your help.

I walk towards him.
Instantly, the air feels
                    breathable.

2

Mr. Nichols cranks up the turntable.

Some record with violins.
Sounds like birds singing.
Chirping almost.
Volume grows.
Becomes quieter.
Fades in and out.

Mr. Nichols has me position the speakers,
                              and adjust some knobs
                to get the balance
                                just right.

Perfection, he says
High-fives me.

Unpack my backpack.
Listening.
Pull out my poems.
Reread them.
For the hundredth time.

Nichols writes on the board—_The Four Seasons_, Vivaldi
Listen for the seasons.

Must be spring, I think hearing more
of the chirping sounds.
Long pause.
New melody.
Don't know this season.
Summer comes after spring.
I'll go with that.

Hi, Calvin.
I'm Sofia.

Hey, Sofia, I say, looking up.
Nice to meet you.

You, too.

Your dad was telling me about you.

Nothing stupid, I hope.

Nope.
I know what she means.
Parents can say some dumb stuff.
Only that we both have Mr. Nichols.

A pause in the music.
Third melody.

What season is this?
Sofia asks.

We listen.

The notes are cascading, she says.

      Nice word, I think.

Like leaves falling.
Must be autumn.

      Must be. I say.

Mind if I sit with you today?

      No problem.
      My face grows warm.
      I look down at the desk.

I wonder if sitting with a girl is cheating on Izzy.
But how can I cheat on someone who's not my friend
                    anymore?

Sofia grabs her backpack.
Hangs it on the chair next to mine.
Sits.

We start our morning work—
Equivalent Fraction Review.

Momma didn't teach this.
Sofia says she learned it last year.
Shows me what to do.
We talk through the problems.
Compare our work.
Music flows—

      cascades—

         in the background.

      What's with the queer music?
      Daniel Walker says to another guy as
         they walk in.

         Queer music.
         Queer teacher,
         the second guy—Jock #2—says.

      That makes two of 'em in one class.

         He's probably got AIDS, too.

I know I'm the other guy they're talking about.
Anyone would know that.

Sofia takes a deep breath.
Sighs.
Looks at me.
Like she thinks I'll say something.
Like she thinks I *should* say something.

Why would they talk bad about Mr. Nichols? I ask.

Why would they talk bad about you?

I'm used to it.

You shouldn't be.

She's right.
Maybe being frozen for so long froze my brain.
Froze my insides, maybe.
Maybe I put up some superhero force field
        to keep the hate out.
But down deep, I know each word,
        each stare,
                each whisper
                        finds its way through
                        the force field
                        like a laser shooting
                        into me.

Did you see their picture in the paper?
Daniel asks the other guy. He shrugs.
Like they're celebrities or something.

I'm the one that sighs this time.
letting the frozenness out
with a puff of warm air.

Turns out
finding
equivalent
fractions
is easy,
but when
it comes
to people,
equivalent
is much
harder
to
find.

3

Show me your poem,

Mr. Nichols says during lunch.
He and Sofia stayed behind
        to eat with me.

I take the notebook from my backpack.
        Pull the stack of poems from
            the front pocket.
        Choose the newest one.
        The one I wrote in bed.
        In the dark.
        Before falling asleep.

Hold it.
Look at it.
Look up at Mr. Nichols.

    No one's ever read
    anything I've written.

Never?

    Nope.

Well today's my lucky day, he says.
I get to enjoy the debut of your writing.

I take a deep breath.
I'm no Langston Hughes, I say,
handing the poem over.

Can I read it out loud? he asks.

Shrug.
Suppose so.

Sofia pulls
a chair
close.

Mr. Nichols
looks
at
the
page.

My heart
pounds
under
my T-shirt.
I look down
to make sure
my shirt's
not moving.

Mr. Nichols leans back.
Reads.
His voice strong.
Growing soft at
the parentheses.
Then louder again.
Back and
forth like a
conversation
between two
people.
Gets to the
last part.

Ashland—the Best Little Town in Florida.
Where my family lives.
Where I grew up.
Where I belonged.
(Until I didn't.)

Mr. Nichols stops.
Looks up.
Does his quiet thing.

> *Powerful,* Sofia says.

> Nice word, I think
> for the second time today.

Nice work,
Mr. Nichols adds.

> *Thanks.*
> I feel a goofy
> grin spreading.

You're right, he continues.
You're no Langston Hughes.

> My grin evaporates.

You're Calvin Johnston.
And that's who you should be.

> The words surprise me.
> Push me back in my chair.

> > *What a strong voice,*
> > Sofia says. *I hear it.*

Agreed.

> *Voice?*
> *I never say anything.*
> *Never what I'm thinking.*

That's not the
kind of voice we mean.

For authors,
voice isn't
only the one
you talk with.
It's also
that thing
that makes
your writing
unique.
Makes it
sound like
you.

> *Wish I could*
> *say it, not just*
> *think it, or write it.*

> > *Agreed,* Sofia says.
> > *I want to do that, too.*

You both
have voice.
And you
both have
voices.
You'll learn to
use them.
No doubt about it.

Sofia and I
do the Nichols-thing.
Sit.
Silent.
Nod our heads.

> *If I ever start saying what I think*
> *I finally say,*
> *I may not be able to stop.*
> *Don't know if Ashland's ready for that.*

This time,
Mr. Nichols and Sofia
nod their heads.
Don't say a word.

4

**Did you hear the one about the three kids who walked into a classroom?
A carrier, a sp . . .**

Stop right there!

Mr. Nichols interrupts Daniel
who's walking in from lunch
with Jock #2.
Their tennis shoes
squawk to a stop.
So do the words spewing
from Daniel's mouth.

*You will not use
that language in
our classroom,*
Mr. Nichols says.

They seem surprised.
Surprised that
anyone heard them.
Surprised that
anyone cared about
what they said.
Surprised that
anyone stopped them.

Whatever, Daniel replies.
Heads to his desk.
Slumps in the chair.
Jock #2 does the same.

Printed on the board—
    Poetry Presentations:
    Sofia
    Calvin
    Marcus

We're the three kids in the joke.
        The carrier,
            and the . . .
                . . . fill in the blanks.

I look at Sofia.
She shrugs.
Shakes her head.
Then I look
at Marcus.

        Don't worry, man,
        he says.
        I'm used to it.

            I've heard it
            all my life,
            Sofia adds.

I nod.
Feel my
jaw
tighten.
I've
used
those
words
too.
Not
to
anyone's
face.
Maybe
not
even
out
loud.

Now to hear the words
roll off someone's
tongue
like it's
the most
normal
thing
to say.

I'm
ashamed.

Not of Daniel
Not of Jock #2.

Of myself.

It's not okay, I reply.

5

I volunteer to go last.

It seems like a good idea.
It isn't.

Marcus goes first.
He's hilarious.
Tells the words his
parents want to hear
him say.
In parentheses,
what he's really
thinking.
Everyone
laughs.
Claps.
Even Daniel
and Jock #2.

Now I'm nervous.
Nothing funny
about my
poem.

Sofia is next.
Can't understand
half of her poem.
Her title tells why.
Mi abuela (My Grandmother).
The poem gives
advice from her
grandmother
in Spanish.
Her words back
to Grandmother
in parentheses and
in English.
Sofia keeps
everyone
leaning
forward,
listening.
I can almost feel
what Sofia feels
even though I don't
know the language.
I can hear
her love for
her grandmother.
I can hear
Sofia's voice.
I'm not nervous anymore.
I'm worried.

No more time
to think about it.
My turn.
I'm up.
Jock #2 coughs.
It's one of those
·coughs that hides
the word you're
saying.
Carrier.
He muffles it,
covering his mouth.
Mr. Nichols
doesn't hear.
I do.
So does Daniel.
He laughs.
I don't.

Enough already,
Sofia says.

What? Daniel replies.
Shrugs.

Enough,
she repeats.

He glares at her.
Slides down in his chair.

I walk to the board.
Turn to face the class.
Sixteen pairs of eyes
focus on me.
Take a deep breath.
Try to remember
how Mr. Nichols
read the poem.
Try to create
his tone with
my voice.
I don't look up.
Just read.
No one laughs.
No one coughs.
It's quiet.
Maybe they're
gonna listen.
Maybe not.

Ashland—the Best Little Town in Florida.
Where kids go to school on weekdays.
Where boys play baseball on Saturdays.
Where families go to church on Sundays.
(Unless you're a kid with HIV.)

Ashland—the Best Little Town in Florida.
Where friends are friendly.
Where everyone is welcome.
Where neighbors are neighborly.
(Unless your skin isn't white.)

Ashland—the Best Little Town in Florida.
Where it's okay to gossip.
Where it's fine to hate.
Where you can treat anyone the way you want.
(As long as they're different than you.)

Ashland—the Best Little Town in Florida.
Where my family lives.
Where I grew up.
Where I belonged.
(Until I didn't.)

I finish.

Stare at the paper
Can hardly believe
I did it—
I read it.
Halfway look up.
Sofia's smiling.
So's Mr. Nichols.
Not Daniel.
He's still slumped down.
Arms folded.
Marcus flashes
two thumbs up.
Jock #2
stares.

I don't care
if anyone claps.
Or if everyone boos.
They can throw eggs
if they want to.
At this moment,
it doesn't matter,
I read a poem.
One of my poems.
Out loud.
In front of
other
people.
My voice
from my
mouth
saying
my words
from my
brain.
And it
didn't
kill
me.

The bees
are buzzing
inside me
again.

And I'm
suddenly
hungry.
Hungry
to
write
more.
Hungry
to
let
my
voice
be
heard.
Hungry
to
read
my
writing
out loud
again.
And
again.
And
again.

6

The end of the day is my favorite part.

Not because it's the end.
But because it's time for
independent work.

Lots of choices—
Read the newspaper
or a favorite book.
Listen to Mr. Nichols' records.
Go to the school library.
Get a head start on homework.
Work in the Writing Center,
or the Science Center,
or the Math Center.

Not a hard choice
for me,
and Sofia,
and Marcus.

We
are
writing
in
no
time.

The Writing Center
has all kinds of paper,
envelopes, a dictionary,
thesaurus, rhyming dictionary,
pencils, pens, even an old typewriter.
Everything I need.
And more.

As I'm getting started,
a paper wad lands on the table.
I don't need to turn around to see who threw it.
Had to be Daniel or Jock #2.
I un-wad the paper.
Read it.

> *If you don't like Ashland.*
> *Get out!*

I wad the paper back up in a ball—tight.
Aim at the trash can.
Throw.

> *Two points!*
> Marcus cheers.

Here's the real point.
Those words
          are garbage to me.

I get back to writing.
My words.
With my voice.
A poem.
For a friend.

7

To Izabelle—

Words.
A dictionary full.
A thesaurus full.
A mind full. A heart full.
Words.
How many are there?
More than I can count.
Sometimes not enough.
Words.
Why can't I say the ones
That fill my thoughts?
That clutter my brain?
Words.
Which words from the dictionary,
And thesaurus, and my brain
Do I say to a friend?
Words.
Of the millions of words that I
Could say, there's only one to give to
My best friend now—
Sorry.

I need to mail a letter,

I tell Officer Lopez,
climbing into the squad car.

> No problem,
> he answers.
> We'll stop by the Post Office.

> Since when do you write letters?
> Curtis asks.

Since today.

I run my hand over
the envelope in my pocket.
The same place I crammed
another envelope a few days ago.

I used a pen to write this poem.
First time ever.
Seemed more serious,
or important,
or permanent
than pencil.

Used one of Mr. Nichols' envelopes.
Had no idea about Izzy's address.
Hope that
            Izabelle Lawrence
            Sandy Beach, Florida
is good enough.

Lopez drives up
to the drop box,
window down.
I hand him the letter.
He looks at me in the mirror.
            Got a stamp?
Hadn't thought of that.
How stupid.

How much are they?

            22 cents, he says.

I don't have a quarter.
Neither does Curtis—
all of his are in the Cuss Jar.
Charlie's are in a
piggy bank at home.
Lopez parks the car
fishes a quarter
from his pocket.
Hands it over.
I go in.

Two people in line.
One at the counter
being waited on by
a woman in a blue uniform.
There are whispers.
Nods in my direction.
I wait.
One person
in line turns.
Leaves.
The customer in
front of me
carries his package
to the counter.
Speaks softly to the
woman working there.
Nods over his shoulder.
Walks out with the
box still under his arm.
I walk up to the window.

The woman in the uniform
slides a sign onto the counter
—CLOSED.
She spins around.
Starts working at
the back counter.

I turn to leave.

Then I remember.
                        I

                    have

                  a

                    voice.

Excuse me,
She doesn't turn around.
Excuse me.
I need a stamp.

        Closed, she snaps.

I need a stamp, please.

        Closed.

This is the Post Office, right?

        She sighs.
        Machine's in the lobby.

Thanks, I answer.

Find the machine.
Drop in the quarter.
It spits out a stamp.
I lick it.
Stick it on the envelope.

Drop the letter in
the Outgoing Mail slot.
Turn to leave.
The man with
the package is
back at the counter.
The CLOSED
sign is gone.

Good news: I used my voice.
               I got what I needed.

Bad news: Nothing much has changed in Ashland.

Not one reporter or camera in sight.

That's what I notice
when we drive up
to the house.

> *There's smoke comin' out of the house!*
> That's what Charlie notices.

> *More like from behind the house,*
> Curtis replies.

A cloud of white-gray
smoke billows
above the back
of the roof.
Where's a reporter
when you need one?

We jump out of the
squad car.
Officer Lopez
doesn't seem worried.
Drives off.
We race around
the house.

Smoke fills the yard.

Hey boys!
Momma calls.

She's in her swimsuit
and flip flops. Shades on
Standing by the grill.
Thick smoke surrounds her.
She clicks a pair of metal tongs.
B.B. tangles around her feet.

What's cooking, Momma?
Curtis laughs at his joke.

Steak and baked potatoes.
she says.
We're celebrating.
Your momma got a job!

The wind shifts.
Blows the smoke at us.
Charlie barks with coughs.
I breathe. Inhale the meaty smell.

That's great, Momma!
I holler.
And it is.
Can't remember the last time we had steak.

Money's been tight.
We've done without
everything but the essentials.

Most days, we can't afford
the essentials either.

Some charity program has
been paying for our doctor bills and meds.
Momma's so embarrassed, she
has me carry the prescriptions
into the pharmacy.
I can feel their stares. Feels like
CHARITY
LOSER
FREELOADER
is written on
my forehead.

Everything else—well, most everything else—has gone
unpaid . . .
water,
electric,
rent.

Unpaid bills are real colorful.
They come with red letters stamped across the
envelopes.
OVERDUE
PAY IMMEDIATELY
FINAL NOTICE

Some un-anonymous friends and even Open Door Fellowship
helped out at first.
Before they really knew what was going on.
Before we got kicked out.
Bought us groceries.
Paid a bill or two.
Brought casseroles over. Lots of casseroles.
That all stopped months ago.
I don't miss tuna casserole one bit.

For a while I had a job delivering newspapers,
but that ended, too—when news got out.
Seems newspaper readers think they
can get AIDS from a paper that's been
tossed in their yard or on their driveway.

Momma never admitted to worrying.
Not when the bills piled up.
Not when bill collectors called.
Not when the power was shut off for four days last November.

I worried enough for both of us.
But Momma made do. Like always.
Saving here. Pinching pennies there.
Doing without luxuries—like steaks and baked potatoes.
Momma's got a job—that makes today an even better day.

Someone go grab the radio,
Momma shouts.
Let's get this party started!

DAY 12
WEDNESDAY
AUGUST 26, 1987

1

Up before the alarm.
Sitting on the porch as the sun comes up.

A dog barks somewhere.
Otherwise, quiet.
Maybe this will be our
                            first
                                        normal day.
That would be a nice change.

I read the poem
I wrote last night
over and over
in the porch light's glow.
Maybe this will be a
                            day as
                                        great as yesterday.
                                                    Maybe even better,
                                                    if that's possible.

When the sun crawls on up,
I see the paint.
Dripping.
Graffiti's back.
Some things
         never
             change.
Me not being okay
        with things that don't change.
                  That's a change.

Alarm rings.
Lights flip on.
The boys are up.

Go to the kitchen.
The phone's unplugged.
Graffiti must not be the only
thing that's come back.

Eat breakfast.
Shower.
Brush my teeth.
Dress.
Comb my hair.
Open the dresser drawer.
Get my poem box—
okay, it's a shoebox.
I'm keeping all my
poems in it.

Stuff last night's poem inside.
Squeeze the box into my backpack.
Grab the sack lunch.
And my brothers.
Climb in the squad car.
Sofia's there.
Drive to school.
No cameras.
No reporters.
Only three protestors.

                  Good change.

Lopez lets us out.
We walk to class.
By ourselves.

                  Another good change.

Some kid waves
at Charlie.
Someone calls
hello to Curtis.

I walk with Sofia.

School's
beginning
to
feel
like
school
again.

Or
to
feel
better
than
school
has
ever
felt
before.

It's an average day.
A normal day.
A good day.

Math.
Science.
Reading.
P.E.
Writing
Social Studies.
Lunch.
Mr. Nichols, Sofia, Marcus, and I
make our own cafeteria.
In our classroom.

Before independent work,
Mr. Nichols lets a few more kids
read poems they wrote.
I listen.
When the last person finishes,
I fish around in my backpack.
Raise my hand.

I have a poem to read, too,
I say.

> *Great!* Mr. Nichols replies.
> Seems surprised.
> Me, too.
> Maybe pleased.
> Me, too.
> *Go ahead,* he says.

The other kids seem okay with it.
Except Daniel.
He sighs. Folds his arms.
Slides down in the chair.
As usual.

I take out the poem.
Walk to the front of the room.
Less nervous than yesterday.
But still nervous.
I've practiced in my own voice.
I almost know it by heart.
Hold tight to the paper.
Just in case.
I begin.

I am the boy with HIV.
But that is not all of me.
I'm a brother.
A poet.
A dreamer.
I'm a beach lover.
And a baseball player.
I'm a son. And a friend to
anyone who'll be a friend to me.

I am the boy with HIV.
But that is not all of me.
I want to date someday.
Maybe even kiss a girl.
I want to graduate from high school.
Maybe go to college.
I want to get married.
Maybe have some kids.

I am the boy with HIV.
But that is not all of me.
Don't look at me
scared of what you think you'll catch.
Look at me
excited for what I have to give.
I listen.
I hear.
I try to understand.
I'm fair.
I'm honest.

I try to treat everyone
the same—no matter
who you are,
or what you are,
or what you're not.

I am the boy with HIV.
But that is not all of me.
I am the boy with HIV.
Please don't let that be all you see.

3

As soon as the bell rings, Jock #2 heads toward me.

Marcus and Sofia
see him coming my way.
They follow.
Stand around me.
Like bodyguards or something.

That was brave, man, he says.

　　　　Thanks, I reply.

I mean it, Calvin, that was really brave.
He turns to
walk away.

Pride fills my chest.
I stand taller.
Try to fight back a smile.

Jock #2 stops.
Turns around.

Walks back.
By the way, he begins,
Pauses.
Sticks out his hand.
Name's Rory.

> I take his hand.
> Look him in the eye.
> He looks back.
> Give a firm grip.
> He does, too.
> Shake.
> *Good to meet you, Rory.*

Sorry for the stuff I said yesterday.
That was stupid.
It won't happen again.
He pauses.
And Daniel will come around.

> *If you say so.*
> My smile's gone.
> But I'm still standing tall.
> Still proud.

He will.
I'll make sure of it.

He walks away.

My bodyguards
stand there.
Mouths open.

What's wrong? I ask.
Like that was the most

normal

thing ever.

4

Office Lopez
comes real close
to adding to the Cuss Jar.

He's never seen stuff like this before.
We have.
We've seen lots of graffiti.
But there is something different about this.
   It wasn't there when we left this morning.
     So it had to be painted in the daylight.
      In full view of anyone who cared.
       No one probably did.

  It's just graffiti,
  Charlie says.

Just graffiti?
Lopez mumbles,
pulling up to
the curb.

Remember when red used
to be my favorite color?
Curtis says.

Red—always in red.
The words cover the entire front of the house.
　　　　Even painted across the windows and door.
All capitals—just in case we didn't notice the message.

DIE ALREADY

This isn't right.
Lopez is still staring
out the car window.
Shaking his head.

Of course
it's not right.
But it's reality.
It's our reality.
Some people in
this town wish I—
wish we—were dead.
They don't just
think it—
they make sure
everyone knows it.

We're out of the car,
examining the dripping paint.

      It's still wet,
      Charlie reports.

By the garage door,
three empty spray paint cans.
I kick at them.
They clank and
clatter against
the driveway
gravel.

The words of my poem
slide into my mind.
I edit the last stanza
in my brain and walk
in front of the house—
from end to end—
whispering the words.

      I am the boy with HIV.
      But that is not all of me.
      I am the boy with HIV.
      And that is all you want to see.

It's just graffiti.
Just.

5

There's no smoke tonight.

No Momma in a bathing suit.
No flip flops and shades.
No steak and baked potatoes.
Momma's in her room.
Listening to U2.
Cassette turned up loud.
Door closed.
That's Momma's way of saying—

Leave me alone.

Phone's ringing.
Probably shouldn't answer.
Momma had it unplugged this morning for a reason.
But it's plugged in now.
I answer.

Tell that woman to stay away.
Except they call Momma something
worse than *that woman.*
We don't want her down here.

Shut your mouth!
I scream into the phone.
Don't you ever say that
word about my Momma.
Slam down the receiver.
I'm panting for breath.
Hands shaking.
Charlie and Curtis stare.

> *Guess that's why Momma's*
> *in her room,* Curtis says.

> Poor Momma,
> Charlie sighs, hugging B.B.
> *Her first day must have*
> *been like our first day.*

Get your homework done, guys,
I say. *I'll fix dinner.*

> *That should be interesting,*
> Curtis replies.

I pull out the last of the food
in the anonymous-friends box.
It'll have to do.
Vienna sausages warmed in a skillet.
Mac and cheese with some extra butter.
Grab the iced tea from the fridge.

Smells decent, Curtis says,
closing his math book.

Charlie pours a bowl of milk for B.B.
Sits it on the floor.

We eat.
No talking.
Muffled music
and cat slurps
are the only sounds
in the kitchen.

After a while,
U2 sounds less muffled.
Louder.
Momma's door must be open.
She comes into the kitchen.
Eyes puffy.
Bloodshot.
She pulls out a chair.
Falls into it like she
can't go one more step.
Charlie leans over.
Hugs her.
Curtis fixes her a plate.
I pour iced tea.

How was work, Momma?
Charlie asks, already knowing
the answer.

> *Well, it's a job,*
> she says,
> *and a paycheck.*

We need that,
I say.
Trying to make her feel better,
or feel different than whatever it is she's feeling

It hurts to see Momma hurt.
Not that she hasn't been hurt before.
But this seems like one of those unfair hurts.
The ones that hurt the most.

> *Doesn't matter.*
> *As long as I'm working.*
> *I'll be in a room by myself.*
> *Filing papers.*
> *A job's a job.*

Rinnnnnggggggg.

Momma's body snaps rigid.
Eyes wide.

> *Unplug that frigging phone,*
> she snaps.

Momma!
Charlie practically yelps.
That's gonna cost you a quarter.

Good thing you've got a job,
Curtis says.

Good try, Curtis, I think.
But it's gonna take
more than a joke
to get Momma
over this funk.

A job's a job.
A paycheck's a paycheck.
Unfair is unfair.
Ashland is Ashland.

The streetlight shines against the window.

The window with letters painted on it.
The light soaks through the sheet.
The sheet that's on the window.
The light pushes the letters—
the letters on the window—
up on the wall.
The wall
across
from
me.

Only two letters fit on the window.
The window covered with a sheet.
Those two letters shove through the glass.
      Through the sheet.
          Pushing their way into my room.
        Into our lives.
          Two letters.
            But they say
            what lots of
            folks still think
            and feel.

DI

Two letters from the window,
up on the wall,
and
into
me.

I want to push my own words through the sheet
out the window
into all of
Ashland.

Rainbow-colored words that drip down every wall,
every window,
every door.

LET US LIVE

DAY 13
THURSDAY
AUGUST 27, 1987

1

**The music of a gospel choir pulls me toward
Mr. Nichols' classroom.**

> *We shall overcome.*
> *We shall overcome.*
> *We shall overcome some day.*

Marcus is already in the room.
Looks through Mr. Nichol's records.
Sofia's unpacking her backpack.

I unpack, too.
Start writing.

Mornin'.

> *Hey, Rory,* I call.

Daniel follows Rory in.
He doesn't follow Rory's lead.
Doesn't speak to anyone.

After morning announcements
and the pledge,
Mr. Nichols begins,
Music is often at the center of a movement.
It can bring people together,
and give voice to a cause.
We're spending today with the
music of the Civil Rights movement.

We listen to music.
Analyze lyrics.
Compare and contrast songs.
Listen to vocal and instrumental versions.

A Change is Gonna Come
People Get Ready
Strange Fruit
Lift Every Voice and Sing
Times They Are a-Changin'
We Shall Not Be Moved

We read about the songs.
Write about them.
Discuss each song's place in history.
Draw the feelings the music stirs in us.
It's all Marcus, Sofia, and I
can talk about at lunch.

The symbolism in Strange Fruit
blows my mind, Marcus says.

Scares me, I say.

Haunting, Sofia adds.

Great word.

I love Lift Every Voice,
Sofia says. *But it almost
seems like a song of celebration.
What was there to celebrate?*

*Maybe they're celebrating
what they know's gonna come,*
Marcus says. *Like a pre-celebration.*

A just-you-wait celebration.
Sofia smiles at the thought.

People Get Ready *is kind of
like that, too. It's my favorite,*
I say. *Gently tells people they'd
better be ready, 'cause change
is coming, whether they like it or not.*

*Are people any different
today than back then?* Marcus asks.

Some are, I guess,
Sofia says.
I hope.

Some aren't, I reply,
thinking of the graffiti
on the house, and how
I used to be like everyone
else in this town.

> *How do people get so*
> *full of prejudice and hate?*
> Marcus asks.

We learn it,
I reply.

> *We?*
> Not only does the word
> come with a question mark,
> Sofia's face is scrunched into
> one, too.

I'm just like everyone
else in Ashland.
I'm prejudiced.
Or I used to be.
I don't want to
be any more.

> *What changed?*
> Another question mark
> on Sofia's face.

I got HIV.

> *Then you were an outcast, too.*
> Marcus slowly nods his head.

Anyone who's
different is
a target
around
here I
guess.

> *Some of us have been targets*
> *not because of what we got,*
> *but just because of*
> *who we are.*

> > *True,* Sofia says.
> > *Both are awful.*

If I didn't have HIV,
do you think I'd be like Daniel?

> *What?* Sofia asks.

I grew up in Ashland,
just like him.
I learned to hate people,
just like him.

Would you have called me that
name Daniel used
and called Marcus the n word?

Not to your face.

Sofia and Marcus stare.

I think I might have.
You know, before.

Before?

Before people started
hating me, too.

Now your family doesn't fit
in any better than mine,
Marcus says.

But I'd never call you
nasty names, Sofia adds.
Not even behind your back.

I let her words sink in.
We haven't always
been outsiders.
We used to be like
everyone else in Ashland.

Everyone who's white.

Right.
Even that didn't
matter once we
got the diagnosis.

Some things have changed, Marcus says.
We're in class together.
We're talking to each other.
Sounds like you've changed, too, Calvin.

Some things have changed, I agree.

But not enough, Sofia adds.

The guy who didn't want
anything to change, nods
his head in agreement.
We eat our lunches.
Listen to the music
pour out of the speakers.

Mr. Nichols sits at his desk.
Humming.

I think about my pact.
My promises to myself.
Keep those promises, I tell myself.
Live those promises.

2

There's one more song I want you to hear,

Mr. Nichols says.
This isn't necessarily a song of the movement,
He Was My Brother *is more of a personal reflection on*
that era.
Give it a listen.

He sits the needle down on the black disk.
Scratch-scratch-scratch
through the speakers.
A guitar, one man's voice,
quickly joined by a second.

I tap my foot.
Feel my body sway with the rhythm.
Then I feel my head tilt.
I lean in closer.
My ears strain to
hear every note.
Every word.

Cursed my brother to his face.
Outsider go home.
This town's gonna be your burying place.
An angry mob trailed along.
And he died so his brothers could be free.

How could this old song—
which has nothing to do
with me or my brothers—
sound like it was written for us?

Cursed my brother—every one of us, and Momma,
        too—*to his face.*
Outsider—me, us—*go home*—as far away as possible.
This town's—Ashland's—*gonna be your burying place.*
An angry mob—PAAS and practically the whole town—
        trailed along.

And he died so his brothers could be free.
Those words scare me.
I try to push them away.
Those words aren't about us.
I'm sure of it.
Doesn't mean anything.
I hope.
Lyrics in a song.
A metaphor.

Dear God, let it just be a metaphor.

3

Your assignment for tonight,

Mr. Nichols says,
Choose a theme song
for your life.
A song that could be the
anthem that would
tell who you are
and what you
stand for.

There are a few moans.
Unfortunately, I can't hide my excitement.

Yes!

Fag.
It's Daniel.

Shut up, Daniel.
Rory snarls.

Don't know if
Daniel means
Mr. Nichols,
or me,
or both
of us.
And
I
don't
think
I
care.

Okay, I do care.
No boy wants to be called that.
No one wants his teacher called that.
No one wants to see someone disrespect someone else.
But what Daniel says doesn't matter now.
I threw his last words in the trash can.
That's where all of them belong.
Daniel Walker will never change.
And my feelings about him . . .

        they don't have to change either.
        Not until he changes.

Leaving the room
after school—
a shove in
my back.

I stumble into
the hall.
Backpack hits the floor.
I do, too.
Look up to see
Daniel.
Glaring.
He spits.
On the floor.
At my feet.
Walks away.
Down the hall.

What's going on?
Mr. Nichols asks,
coming out the door.

> *Same ole same ole,* I reply.
> *Some people will never change.*

His hand reaches down
to help me up.
But some people are changing . . . a lot,
Mr. Nichols says.

I'm glad he noticed.

4

**I wonder if Izzy would love this theme-song thing
as much as me.**

She'd know all kinds of
tunes to choose from.
She'd probably find the perfect song.
The one I would hear and
say—*Yeah, that's you.*
Maybe she'd choose something
old and twangy from Patsy Cline.
Or something jazzy from Billie Holiday.
Or maybe the Beatles.
Or something classical.
Or something playing on K-I-C-K—
Momma's favorite radio station.

I start my search.
Need a song that fits me.
Something that tells what I stand for.
What *do* I stand for?
Family, I guess.
Has to be a song that tells about my life.

Illness?
I'm more than that.
Death?
Too depressing.
Being a big brother?
I am that.
Change?
I do know a thing or two about that.

Wonder who Izzy thinks she is
and what she thinks
she stands for.
Wonder who she thinks I am
and what she thinks
I stand for.
Wonder what song
she would think
would be
the
perfect
song
for
me.

Of course, she's never thought
about it and couldn't care less.

I
wonder
what
song
I
think
is
the
perfect
song
for
me?

And if Izzy will
ever be willing
to listen to it.

5

Officer Lopez asks as
we climb in the squad car.
Before Sofia and I can answer . . .

Terrible, Charlie moans.
The worst, Curtis says.

Why? I ask.
What happened?

Mrs. McKnight still calls me Charles,
Charlie said. *And she won't
get near my papers, or my
drawings, or anything I touch.
Stands over me and looks
at them, but she won't touch them.*

That's awful,
Sofia replies.
She turns around
from the front seat
to look at him.

374

I'm sorry, Charlie, I say.

Thanks, he mumbles.

*Mrs. Warden's class is more
like a prison now.
And the inmates are
running wild,* Curtis says.
*Everyday someone tries
to pick a fight,
cusses at me,
throws something.
Every frigging day.*

*Curtis, you've never fought back
once,*
I say. *Why?*

I'm not giving up my power.

Your what? Sofia asks.

*My power. I heard it on a TV show.
If you do something because of
someone else,
then they have all the power, not you.
I'm keeping all my power for myself.*

Good for you, Curtis, I say.
And I mean it.

Officer Lopez shakes his head
Hang in there boys, he says.
Things are bound to get better—
sooner or later.

        I'm betting on later,
        Curtis replies.

There's no more talking
the rest of the drive.
Don't dare say I had
another good day—
except for some spit on my shoes.

Officer Lopez pulls up to the curb.
      Look at our house! Charlie cheers.
        Looks brand new from top to bottom,
        says Curtis.
          Who did that? I ask.

A little project on my day off,
Officer Lopez answers.

        Sofia is smiling from ear
        to ear.
        I had the hardest time
        keeping the secret all
        day.
        I picked out the color.

It's almost the color of your hair,
I say.

Maybe, she replies.

My new favorite color, Curtis says.
Thanks, Officer Lopez.
Thanks so much.

You're welcome, Calvin, Lopez answers.
I thought it was time for a fresh start.
Let's see them try to paint over that.

He turns off the engine.
Looks into the rearview mirror.
Boys, Officer Lopez begins,
your momma's had a hard day, too.
The newspaper let her go.

Let her go? Charlie repeats.

They fired her, I explain.

Why?

Too many complaints from workers
and subscribers is what they told her,
he explains.

Nothing ever changes
in this stupid town, Curtis mumbles.

I was thinking a lot of
things *had* changed.
I was thinking things
~~were different~~
Were better.
I was thinking it was another
fantastic day at school.
The best school year ever.
I was thinking I'd
found some friends.
I was thinking I'd
found a teacher I like.
But now I'm thinking
that might not be enough.

Miss Kissinger took
your Momma into Tampa
for dinner and a movie,
Officer Lopez says.
To try to cheer her up.

What about us? Charlie asks.

Your Mom's ordered pizza.
Left money on the cabinet.
Said to do your homework
And get to bed by 9:00.

My home number's on the kitchen table.
Call my wife if you need anything.
I'm on duty tonight.
I'll keep a watch on the house.

Got it, I reply.
No worries.

But I have to face facts.
The Blood Brothers
still have lots
to worry
about,
and
a lot
more
things
need
to
change.

Normal pizza routine.

Cash on the porch.
Knock on the door.
Pizza left behind.
We eat.
Feed the cat.
Lopez honks each time
he drives by.
Do homework.
Brush teeth.
Watch the tube.
Eat some snacks.
Not in bed by 9:00.
Make it by 10:00.
Me and my brothers—
my blood brothers—
crowd into our
room.
They sleep.
Maybe they dream.

Maybe they hope that
tomorrow
will be
the day
when
the day
is good
for all
of us.

I write.
To try to find the good.
To try to remember the good.
To try to hold on to the good.

DAY 14
FRIDAY
AUGUST 28, 1987

1

**Lopez must be driving by a lot.
Keeps honking.**

And I must have slept in.
Light from the window
warms my face.
Roll over.
Breathe in deep.
Start coughing.
My nostrils burn.
My throat tightens
into another cough.
      And another.
          And another.
Charlie's coughing, too.

Honk! Honk! Honk!

Sniff at the air.
Smoke?

I sit up in bed—
hit my head on the
bottom of Charlie's bunk.
Is Momma cooking outside again?
For breakfast?
My mind is hazy—
only half-awake.
White streams of smoke
sneak in around
the edges of the
curtain sheet.
Swirl around
the floor.
Float up to
the ceiling.

Honk! Honk! Honk!

Rub my eyes.
A spark of fear ignites
somewhere inside me.
Is this another movie dream?
I swing my legs out of bed.
Sit up. Sparks of fear turn
into flames of terror.

Orange glow fills
the room.
F-L-A-M-E-S.

I shout the word
as soon as I
think it,
FLAMES!
FIRE!

The words choke on
smoke and barely
make a sound.
Flames in front
of the window.
The window covered
by the sheet-curtain.

Honk! Honk! Honk!

FIRE! I scream. **FIRE!**

2

Curtis is up in a flash.
Grabs Charlie from bed.

I yank on a pair of shorts.
Grab my backpack.
Throw it on my shoulders.
Stupid.
I know.
Stupid
Should escape. Run.
But my poems are in that backpack.
My voice.
My life.
I reach for the door knob.
Wrap my hand around it.

Ah-h-h-h-h!

Searing pain.
The doorknob
burns into my flesh.

Ah-h-h-h-h!

My scream won't stop,
but I don't let go.
Turn the knob.
Throw open the door.
Black smoke
rolls in.
We crouch low
to the floor.
Scorching heat
pushes in right
behind the smoke.
Curtis coughs.
Charlie coughs more.
Down the hall,
flames lick up
the walls of the
living room.
The curtains
evaporate in
an orange blaze.

Back door,
I yell.

> *Stay low,*
> Curtis shouts.

I remember it
from scouts, too.
Smoke rises.

Cleaner air
lower down.
He pulls Charlie
down with him.
Curtis in front.
Charlie in the middle.
I follow.
We crawl on the carpet.
It melts toward us.

What's happening?
Charlie screams.

Where's Momma?
Curtis yells.

We crawl by her
open bedroom door.
Smoke fills every
inch of the room.
Bed's made.

Maybe she's still out.

Maybe she's in the living room.

I look ahead.
The living room
is now all flames.
Yellow, orange, red

flames that eat up
everything around them.
I hope Momma's still out.
The thought that she might
not be turns my flames
of fear into a raging wildfire.

Faster! Faster!
I yell.

An explosion of glass
rains down on us.
I tuck my head.
Look behind.
Flames are spreading
from our bedroom,
up the hall, crawling
toward us.
Flames in front.
Flames behind.

Hurry! I scream. *Hurry!*

We crouch and crawl.
Coughing. Choking.
My eyes burn.
Heat blasts my face.
The smoke is
thicker. Blacker.

I can barely see
Charlie's feet
in front
of me.
Can't see
Curtis
at all.
He and Charlie turn right.
Into the kitchen.
I follow.
If you can crawl
and run at the same
time, we do.

Almost to the back door
Yank off my T-shirt.
Wrap it around my hand.
Pain shoots through me
again. ***Ah-h-h-h-h-h!***
Crawl over Charlie.
Push Curtis aside.
Grab the knob.
More hot pain.
But not as intense.
The T-shirt helps.
Turn the knob.
Push.
Nothing.
Locked.

Fire! Curtis yells.
Right behind us.

Reach for the old deadbolt.
Click.
The new deadbolt.
Clii k
Turn the knob again.
Pull hard.
The door opens.
Air rushes in.
Shove Charlie and Curtis out.
Follow behind them.
We tumble onto wet grass.
Another explosion.
Glass from the kitchen
window rains down
on us like handfuls of
sand during pretend war.
Flames dance along
the window frame and
around the door.
The door we
came through
seconds ago.

Sirens wail.
Dogs bark.
We cough.
A lot.

Gasp for breath.
The familiar night sky—
the Big Dipper,
the Little Dipper,
the North Star—
looks down on
three brothers
Alive.
Barely.

My brothers pant beside me.

The wet grass soaks through
my shorts. Curtis' shorts and
T-shirt must be sopping wet, too.
Charlie's in his Superman
underwear and T-shirt.
We could have used
Superman tonight.
But we survived.
All by ourselves.
Without a
super
hero.

I gulp in lungs-full of fresh air.
Try to unwrap the T-shirt.
It feels stuck.
Even touching the fabric
sends a shockwave
of pain through
my fingers
and palm.

Pain
  throbs,
     throbs,
        throbs
with each
   beat,
      beat,
         beat
           of my heart.

Blood Brother roll call.
I say.
Curtis?

        Present and accounted for.

Charlie?
        Here.

I know they're here.
But I want to hear
their voices. To
make my mind
know we're
alive.

        B.B.! Charlie gasps.

We forgot B.B.
He was curled up

with Charlie in the top bunk.
In our panic.
we never
thought
about the
little
guy,

He'll find a way out, Curtis says.
Tries to sound like he means it.

We've got to get him.
We've got to save him.

No, I say.

But we have to, Charlie says.

NO! And that's final.
My voice sounds
like Momma's or Officer Lopez'.
Strong. In charge.
Like the man
of the family.

No one's going back in that house,
I say.
No one.

Charlie curls into a ball.
Cries into the grass.
        B.B., he calls.

       He'll make it, Curtis says again.

I shake my head.
Try to let Curtis know
lying isn't gonna make
the situation any better.

I'm sorry, Charlie, I say.
But the three of us are safe.
That's what's important.

        B.B., B.B., he cries
        over and over.

4

Sweet Jesus!* Momma screams. *My boys! My boys!

Sirens harmonize with her screams.
Blue lights flash round and round
tossing their glare into the sky,
over the house,
into the backyard.

My boys! Momma screams.
Calvin! Curtis! Charlie!
Oh, my God! Oh, my God!
Where are they?

> *We're here, Momma.*
> I yell.
> Sirens drown out my voice.

I grab Charlie's hand, pull him up.
Curtis jumps to his feet.
We run around the house.
Officer Lopez is kicking
in the front door.

A blast of flames
throws him off
the porch,
to the ground,
on his back.

Firetruck pulls up
behind the squad car.
An ambulance close behind.
Red flashing lights converge
with the blue ones.

A paramedic rushes to Lopez.
Another comes in our direction.
Firemen pull on their gear.
Unroll hoses, hook up to the hydrant.

Momma's on her knees.
Head on the ground.
Her shoulders heaving
up and down.
Mandy Kissinger
is beside her.
Hand on Momma's back.

>   *Momma!* Charlie calls.
>   He runs to her.
>   Wraps her in a hug.

Momma looks up.
Sees us—screams again—
Boys! My boys!

    B.B.'s missing.
    Charlie says.
    We've got to find him

I'm sorry, baby,
Momma says.
We'll get you another cat.
We've got each other—
that's all that matters.

    No it's not.
    What about B.B.?
    He's part of the family, too.
    He's a Blood Brother.

The paramedic
reaches our huddle.
Carries a metal tool box.
Everyone ok?

    I hold up my T-shirt-covered hand.
    Burned it on the doorknob, I say.

Let me take a look, he says.
Puts down the tool box, walks toward me.

Got HIV, I say.
Better glove up.

Thanks for telling me.
I will, he answers.
Pops open the box.
Takes out gloves.
Pulls them on.
Then snaps on
                          a second pair.
Gently takes my hand.
I wince. Pain shoots through me.
He examines the stuck shirt.
Better let a doc take care of this,
he says. You're gonna need some
pain meds. We'll take you to the ER.

Lopez is sitting up now.
Oxygen mask strapped
to his face.

Firemen tug and
drag hoses.
Position them.
They fatten, expand.
Water snakes its
way through them.
Then bursts out.
Spraying the house.
Spraying through the door.

Spraying in our bedroom window.
It doesn't help.
Flames grow.
        Spread.
                Engulf.
                        Destroy.

Charlie? Momma says.
Where's Charlie?

        He was standing right here,
        Curtis replies, looking around.

      B.B., the thought falls from
      my brain out of my mouth.

Oh, God, no.
Momma hollers.
Did he go back in the house?

Officer Lopez pulls the
oxygen mask off his face.
Didn't come this way,
he puffs.
Stumbles up on his feet.

Flames pour out the door.
Shoot out the windows.
Spread through the roof.
Smoke rolls

into the sky.
Firemen yank
the hoses
around the house.

          Maybe he's in back, I say.

We race to the backyard.

          Charlie!
               Charlie! Curtis and I scream.

Oh dear, God.
Oh dear, God,
Momma cries over and over and over.
My baby! My baby!

          CHARLIE! CHARLIE!

I scream louder than the sirens.
Louder than Momma's cries.
Louder than I knew my voice could scream.

          CHARLIE!

5

The firemen shoot a blast of water into the back door.

Two of them enter
the house through
the spraying water.
Into the smoke.
Into the flames.

Mandy's got her arm
around Momma.
Lopez joins us.
Puts a hand on
Curtis' shoulder.
And mine.

I'm shaking my head.
Charlie, Charlie, Charlie,
I mumble,
         or chant,
                  or pray.
I had us all out.
Safe.
Charlie, Charlie, Charlie.

The sirens are off now.
The sound of crackling flames,
        breaking glass,
           and Momma's cries fill
           the night.

We wait.
    And wait.
        And w-a-i-t.

      Where are they? Curtis asks.
      Shouldn't they be out by now?

A figure appears in the smoke.
    Comes through the doorway.
        A firefighter—coughing, choking.
          Falls gasping to the ground.

        Medic! Lopez hollers.
          Rushes to the firefighter.

A second figure in the doorway.
    Carries something—something limp.
      Something cradled in his arms.
        Something blackened by smoke.

The firefighter places
a limp, soot-covered
body on the ground.

Collapses beside it.
Gasps for breath.
The body doesn't move.

CHARLIE!
Momma screams.

This scream is different than
the other screams.
It's bigger than all the
others combined.
It's a scream that
sends shivers through me.
Rips into my heart.
Pushes tears out of my eyes.

A paramedic runs to Charlie.
Bends over him.
His ear to Charlie's mouth.
Pushes down in the center
of his superhero covered chest.
Counts.

1 . . . 2 . . . 3 . . . 4 . . . 5 . . . 6 . . .

His counts are fast.
Steady.

7 . . . 8 . . . 9 . . . 10 . . . 11 . . . 12 . . .

We gather close.
Momma's hands folded.

> *Please, God. Please,* she begs.

> *13 . . . 14 . . . 15 . . . 16 . . . 17 . . . 18 . . .*

Come on, Charlie, I say.

Mandy wraps her hands
on top of Momma's.

> *19 . . . 20 . . . 21 . . . 22 . . . 23 . . . 24 . . .*

> *Damnit, Charlie!* Curtis screams.
> *Breathe! Breathe!*

> *25 . . . 26 . . . 27 . . . 28 . . . 29 . . . 30 . . .*

The paramedic changes positions.
Tilts Charlie's head.
Lifts his chin.
Pinches his nose.
Leans toward his mouth.

> *He's got HIV,* Momma yells.
> Her boy may be dying,
> and she still has to worry.
> About HIV.

The paramedic pauses for a second.
Like thoughts are going through his brain.
Takes his hands away.
Leans back on his heels.

> *What's he doing?* Momma whispers.
> Nothing.
> He's not doing a
> damn thing.

Do something, I scream.

The paramedic looks down
at Charlie.
Then looks at his own hands.
It's like I see the
thoughts
spinning
in his
brain.
He's thinking he's
got it
now.

Lopez rushes over.
Pushes the guy out of the way.
Lifts Charlie's chin again.
Puts his mouth on Charlie's mouth.
Blows hard.

Charlie's chest rises.

                Falls.

He blows again.
Rise.

       Fall.

1 . . . 2 . . . 3 . . . 4 . . . 5 . . . 6 . . .

The whole thing starts again.
With Lopez doing the pushing.

The second paramedic—
the one with double gloves—
pushes a stretcher into
the backyard.
Bumps over ruts and hoses.
Parks it next to Charlie.
The first guy goes to Charlie's feet.
The paramedic with the stretcher
positions himself next to Charlie's head and shoulders

On the count of three, he says.

Lopez continues.
To count. To push.

7 . . . 8 . . . 9 . . .

1, 2, 3. Lift.

They lift Charlie onto the stretcher.
    Latch the wheels.
        Carry the stretcher out of the yard.
        Lopez walks beside.
        Still pushing, still counting.

        Carolyn, he calls.
        Ride in the ambulance with Charlie.
        Mandy, bring the boys.

        28 . . . 29 . . . 30 . . .

He leans forward.
Breathes two large breaths again.

    Rise.
        Fall.
    Rise.
        Fall.

Back to pushing and counting.
They lift the stretcher into the ambulance.
Lopez still counting.
Still pushing.
Still breathing.
Momma climbs in.
Grabs Charlie's hand.

Doors slam.
Siren screams.

I see Momma's face through the window.
        White.
Eyes staring at our blazing house.
        Shakes her head.
Leans down.
        Kisses Charlie's forehead.

We climb into Mandy Kissinger's car.
She speeds after the ambulance.

I reach out my hand.
Place it on top of Curtis's hand.
His fingers wrap around mine.
Blood Brothers, I whisper.
        Blood Brothers, he replies.

From the car window,
I see him.
Sitting
alone
at the end
of the driveway.
Watching us.
B.B.

Must be that
cats-with-nine-lives thing.
Lucky cat.
I've got a brother
with only one life.
He needs all the luck he can get.

But if B.B. can make it,
then Charlie can, too.
Right? I say to the window.

I look again.
B.B. is gone.

Mandy Kissinger drives fast.

We pull in right behind the ambulance.
She swerves into the nearest parking space.
Curtis and I are out before the car stops.

Lopez is still pushing, counting, breathing
when the stretcher's unloaded from the ambulance.

Doctors and nurses rush out.
Quick conversation
with the paramedics.
     7-year-old male.
     HIV.
     Smoke inhalation.
     CPR performed for 18 minutes.
A nurse takes over.
Pushing.
     Counting.
          Breathing.
But Lopez stays with Charlie.

The stretcher's rolled through the sliding doors.
Down the hall.
   Around a corner.
    Disappears.

Momma's still sitting.
In the ambulance.
I reach for her.
She reaches back.
Curtis and I help her out.
She makes it to a bench
outside the hospital doors.
Sits. Puts her head in her hands.

It's my fault, she says.

   No, Momma.
   You couldn't have done anything, I say.

   It's all because of that damn cat,
   Curtis swears.

We should have left this town ages ago.
But I had to fight. I had to try to prove a point.
It wasn't worth it. It wasn't worth it at all.

   No, Momma, it's not your fault, I say again.
   I know it's not.
   Because it's my fault.

I'm supposed to be the man of the family—
Dutch said so.
I had everyone out safe,
but I didn't keep my eyes on Charlie.
I said I was okay with change.
I stopped fighting it.
Now the biggest change ever
has blazed its way right into our lives.
It's all my fault—but I can't find a voice to say it.

7

I've already been through the HIV stuff with the woman who checked me in at the emergency room, every nurse I've seen, and the doctor.

My hand is still throbbing.
I hold my arm at the elbow.
Trying to keep it steady.
Trying to not let anything touch it.
Trying to will the pain away.

Momma's in a room down the hall.
Waiting.
Seems like forever.
I didn't want to leave her.
Doctor said I had to.
Curtis came with me.
Momma said he had to.

We don't say anything.
    Not about the fire.
        Not about our escape.
           Not about Charlie.

One side of my brain says:
    Come on Charlie.
    You can do this.

The other side of my brain says:
   Come on Charlie.
   We need you to do this.

The doctor gloves up.
Says, Take this.
Hands me a little cup.
One pill inside.

   I don't wanna be knocked out, I reply.

It won't knock you out.
It will lessen the pain. Trust me.
You'll be glad you took it.

I take the pill.

She positions my hand over a bowl.
Opens a bottle of clear liquid.
Almost instantly, the meds
take hold. They don't knock
me out, but I feel like I'm
swimming under water
or something.

Saline solution, the doctor says.
Sterile. Safe.

   Saline? Isn't that salt? That's gonna hurt.

Thanks Curtis, I reply.

No, the doctor says.
*Salt water would sting.
Not saline solution.*

She pours the solution
over the shirt
covering my hand.
It begins to soak in.
Liquid drips into the bowl.

The shirt's kept the wound clean,
she says. *That was smart.*

        I wasn't trying to be smart, I admit.
        I was trying not to get burned again.

She keeps pouring.
Cool wetness touches my skin.
I can't decide if it's the saline solution,
or my foggy, underwater brain.
Before long, the entire T-shirt is wet,
my hand relaxes in the dampness.

        How much longer is this going to take? I ask.
        I gotta get back to my mom. My brother.

*Not long.
Your brother's in good hands.*

Slowly she begins to unwind the shirt
I stiffen.
Anticipating the pain.
The pill must do more
than make me water-brained.
I feel a gentle tug as the
fabric pulls at the burned skin.
The shirt comes off.
I don't scream or do anything else embarrassing.

My fingers are covered with blisters.
Skin peeling off.
My palm is red. No blisters.
I don't feel the throbbing.
But by the look of the blisters, I bet I will.

Gross.

Thanks, again, Curtis.

Second degree burns, the doctor says.
Stands to leave.
The nurse will finish up.
I'll leave a prescription for meds.

The nurse gloves up.
Pours more solution over my hand.

Keeping the wound clean is essential, she says.

Okay. Got it. Willing her to hurry.

She spreads on greasy, white goo.
Wraps my hand with gauze,
I look like something from the
mummy exhibit at the history museum.

By the time she finishes up,
the pain is back.

Nurse hands me the prescription.
The hospital pharmacy can fill it, she says.
Check in with your doctor ASAP.

We can go now. Right?

Nope. Doctor's ordered a transfusion.

I didn't lose any blood.

Doctor's orders, she says.
Walks out of the room.

But . . .

A transfusion.
That's what started
all of this to begin with.
The last thing I want is

someone else's blood inside me,
pumping through my veins.

> *Shut up, and get the transfusion,*
> Curtis says, like he can hear the
> conversation in my head.
> *We got to have you well, Calvin.*
> *Can't take any chances.*
> *We can't have two Blood Brothers down.*

I lean back as the nurse
pushes the needle in my
arm, hangs the bag on
the rack above my head.
Watch as the slow drip
from the bottle, runs
Into the tube, and into
my body.

I can't complain.
It's not difficult. It's not painful.
I hope that the same is true
    for whatever Charlie
        is going through right now.

8

Arson. I hear the word from across the room.
Someone tells Lopez.
Gas cans outside the bedroom window.

> **ar·son**
> /ˈärs(ə)n/
> *noun*
> 1. the criminal act of deliberately setting fire
>   to property.

Never thought it
was an accident.
But hearing the word—
ARSON—
makes my skin crawl.
Makes me want to throw up.

Someone set fire
to our house.
Outside our
bedroom window.
Outside the window
where we slept.
Where three kids slept.

They
had to
know
we
were
inside.

They weren't trying to scare us,
                  or warn us,
                        or get us to leave.

They.Were.After.Blood.
They.Wanted.Us.Dead.

The little windowless room gets smaller and smaller.

Some hospital woman
put us in a private waiting room.
Don't know if she was keeping people from us,
or us from people.

Mandy Kissinger comes in.
No camera. No clipboard.
Officer Lopez arrives
with Mrs. Lopez.
He stands guard
outside the door.
Every now and then
his radio squawks.

Each time
the door
opens,
Momma
looks up.
Expecting
news.
I do, too.

So far,
no
news.

The door opens again.
More expectation.
It's Mr. Nichols.

*I told the school I had to
come,* he says.
Shakes Momma's hand.
*Told them someone would
have to cover our class.*
Tells Momma how sorry he is.
Shakes Mrs. Lopez's hand, too.
Turns to me.

I stand.
Reach out my hand.
He reaches out his.
Grabs hold.
Pulls me to him.
Hugs me.
Holds me tight.
All the fear.
All the terror.
All the worry.
Pour out of me.
I cry into his shirt.
A silent cry.

A shoulder-shaking cry.
His tears
drop down
on my head.
Mix with mine.

> *I'm so sorry, Calvin.*
> he whispers.
> *No one should ever be*
> *treated the way you and your*
> *family have been treated. No one.*

It's all my fault,
I whisper.

> Mr. Nichols takes me by the shoulders.
> Pushes me back a bit.
> Looks me in the eyes.
> *Calvin, none of this is your fault.*
> *Hate is to blame. Not you.*

I collapse back into him.
More tears soaking his shirt.
More silent, shoulder-shaking sobs.
Minutes pass.
I don't know how many.
I wipe my face.
Introduce Mr. Nichols to Curtis.

The door opens again.
Momma's face lights up with expectation.
A doctor comes in.
Officer Lopez behind him.
Shuts the door.
Momma's look of expectation
slowly
melts
away.

10

The doctor sits down across from Momma.

He looks serious.
Doctors always do.

Momma's already shaking
her head. Whispering.
No. No. No.

I'm sorry, he says.

No. No. No.

Smoke is more dangerous than fire.
Like he's a scout master delivering a talk.
We did CPR for nearly two hours.

No. No. No.

We couldn't bring him back, Mrs. Johnston.
I'm so sorry. We couldn't bring him back.

Charlie, she wails. *Charlie.*

I grab hold of Momma.
So does Curtis.
We hold on to each other.
Like we have nothing else to hold on to.
'Cause we don't have anything else to hold onto.
The pain in my hand is replaced by a different
            searing pain.
A pain so bad, so deep, I don't think I can stand it.

Arms wrap around us.
They hold us, too.
A circle of tears.
A circle of sorrow.
A circle of grief.
A circle without Charlie.

11

I'm sorry, Mrs. Johnston, some hospital woman says.

Everyone's sorry.
Now.
Now they're sorry.
Now.
Too little. Too late.

We have to take care of some business before you go.
How would you like the remains to be handled?
she says to Momma.

> *Remains?* I say.
> *His name is Charlie.*
> *He's not remains.*
> *He's a boy*
> *He's my brother.*

I'm sorry, the woman says again.
Looks at me.
Looks like she really means it.
Looks back at Momma.
How would you like Charlie to be handled?
What arrangements do you want us to make?

Arrangements.
I understand the words.
But not what she means.

Cremation, Momma says.

The word hits me
between the eyes.

Momma? I say.

Charlie just died.
In a fire.
And we're going to cremate him?

Momma, are you sure?

I want Charlie cremated.
Momma says it again.
Like she's trying to explain.
To me.
To the woman.
To everyone in the room.
To herself, maybe.
We're gonna take his ashes to the beach.
Charlie loves the beach,
she says to Mrs. Lopez.

Changes one word.
Charlie loved the beach.

Then there's the matter of
the emergency room
and cremation bill, the woman says.

You've got to be kidding me,
Curtis snaps.
Our brother has died, and
you want money?

Hush, Curtis,
Momma says.
It's her job.
Ma'am we've not
got any insurance.

The newspaper will
take care of it,
Mandy Kissinger says.

Momma looks up at her.
A question mark on her face.

I've already called the
editor-in-chief.
The newspaper will pay
for everything.
Mandy Kissinger looks
at me like she
thinks she knows
what I'm thinking, and
continues.
We're not expecting
anything in return.
It's exactly what I was
thinking.

Momma signs papers.
Curtis paces the room.
Mandy Kissinger hugs Momma,
says she'll be back later.
Back where?
Here at the hospital?
No. We'll be leaving here.
Back at our house?
It's not there anymore.
Where do we live?
Where do we go back to?

12

**As Momma finishes up with the hospital lady,
Rev. Walker from Open Door Fellowship walks in.**

The preacher goes straight to Momma.
Gets down on one knee.
Looks her in the eye.
Shakes his head.
Sad look on his face.

> *Carolyn, I am so sorry for your loss,* he says.
> *It's all part of God's plan.*

Momma's face trembles.
Silent tears pour out of her eyes.

> *The congregation and I want to
> minister to you in your hour of need.*

Our hour of need? I say.

Rev. Walker turns to look at me.

> *Yes, Calvin. Grief is a terrible thing
> to experience. Only with God's help
> can we make it through such a thing.*

Something begins to burn in me.
Heat. Growing. Spreading.
From my heart.
To my brain.
To my mouth.

Reverend, our hour of need has
been going on for over a year.
Where have you been?

His head shakes a little, his eyelids flutter.
Surprise on every part of his face.

How can you say
this is part of God's plan?
Hate is part of God's plan?
Disease is part of God's plan?
A little kid dying is part of God's plan?

The reverend shakes his head again.

If that's your God, I don't need him.

He looks over at Momma.
Back at me.

We've got by without you and your
church all this time.
And we'll do fine without you now.

Carolyn, he says, taking Momma's hand, *the boy's upset.*
Momma pulls her hand away.
I know he doesn't mean what he's saying.

> *You're damn right he's upset.*
> Curtis says. *We all are.*
> *But Calvin means every word he says.*
> *He's speaking for all of us.*

Momma nods in agreement.

There might be a church out there
that can minister to us, Reverend Walker.
But it won't be your church.
Like you said, you only get through
something like this with God's help.
He'll be all we need for now.

I stand up.
Cross to the reverend.
Stick out my hand.
Look him in the eye.
He stands to his feet.
Doesn't stick out his hand.
Curtis opens the door.

We'll pray for you
and your church, I say.
I point to the door.

13

The preacher's gone, Momma's signing the last of the papers for the hospital.

What time is it?

> *2:00 in the afternoon, Calvin,*
> Officer Lopez answers.
> *You all have been here for over twelve hours.*

Is there a phone I can use? I ask.
Officer Lopez walks me down
to the nurse's desk.
Asks the nurse for me.
She gets up.
Lets me have her seat.
I pick up the receiver of her phone.

I dial the number.
Ring.
> Ring.
> > Ring.

> *Hello?*

Izzy?
I fight away tears.
Hold my voice steady.

> *Calvin. I'm glad you called.*
> *Thank you for the poem.*
> *It just came in the mail.*
> *We have a lot of talking to do.*

You're welcome.
I really need to
talk to you, too.

> *Calvin, everything's going to be okay.*
> *Next time you come to the beach*
> *we'll be our old selves again.*
> *Everything will be back to normal.*

Izzy, Charlie's dead.
I blurt it out.
Can't keep from it.

> *What? You're not serious?*
> *Don't joke around.*

I'm not joking.

> *No! No! How? What happened?*

A fire. Arson.
We're at the hospital.

> *No, Calvin. It can't be.*

Izzy, I need to talk to Gramps.

> *Oh, Calvin. I can hear her tears.*
> *Not our Charlie.*
> *Gramps, she calls.*

I hear a muffled sound.
Her hand on the phone I guess.
Seconds pass.
More muffled sounds.
Then Gramps' voice.

Mr. Lawrence. It's Calvin Johnston.
I need your help.

> *Calvin, do they know how it happened?*
> *How's your mother? Is anyone else hurt?*

Arson.
Ashland did it, Mr. Lawrence.
All of Ashland did it.
We're hurt.
All of us.
Hurt real bad.

Calvin, I'll do anything I can.

We're coming to the beach.
It's where Momma wants to take Charlie.
Mr. Lawrence . . .
I pause. Take a deep breath.
Like I haven't breathed all day.
Mr. Lawrence, I need Izzy.
I need my best friend.
I can't get through this without her.
We all need her, Mr. Lawrence.
Will you let us be friends again?

There's silence.
I breathe deep again.
I can hear my heart
        beating in my ears,
            throbbing in my hand.

I'm an old fool. Calvin. A damn fool, Izzy would
say.
I won't do anything to keep you two apart.
Promise. You have my word.

Thank you, Mr. Lawrence.
We'll see you all sometime tomorrow.

And Calvin . . .

Yes, sir.

> *I want you to call me Gramps*
> *Like always.*

Like always, I repeat.
Thanks, Gramps.

14

**Your Momma's settled in the guest room, Officer
Lopez says.**
Hope you boys are okay on the sleeper sofa.

We're good, I say.

> Thanks for letting us stay the night, Curtis adds.

Wouldn't have it any other way, Lopez replies.
He switches off the light.
Heads down the hall.
Curtis flops around till he's comfortable.
I roll my pillow up behind my neck.

> What will we do without him?
> Curtis says into the dark.

I don't know, I answer.
Guess we keep living.

> It's not fair, Calvin.
> It's not fair that it was Charlie.
> I wish it had been me instead.

I was wishing it had been me.

> What's gonna come of Momma?

We have to take care of her the best we can.
She's gonna need us more than ever.

The room is quiet. Dark.
B.B. curls up beside me.
Sophia found him.
Brought him home.
Cleaned him up.
Now he's curled up
between Curtis
and me.
A small
warm
body
where
Charlie's
small
warm
body
should
be.

Curtis' breathing is steady.
Like he's fallen asleep.
My body's tired.
My hand aches.
My eyes are heavy.
Drifting . . . off to . . . sleep . . .
Just before I do . . .

Good night, Charlie, I whisper.

DAY 1—WITHOUT CHARLIE
SATURDAY
AUGUST 29, 1987

1

Mandy Kissinger's driving us down 1-75 by 8:50 a.m.

Everyone's supposed
to be at the beach by
10:00.

Don't know if I can do this,
Momma says.
Don't know if I can let him go.

> *One day at a time,* Mandy Kissinger says.
> *That's all you can do.*

Maybe one minute at a time, Momma replies.

Curtis and I are in the back seat.
B.B. naps between us.
Hardly seems fair.
B.B. made it.
Charlie didn't.

My fingers brush across
the kitten's head.
Lots of things aren't fair, of course.

My brother and I stare out opposite windows.
Wonder if Curtis is thinking what I'm thinking.
Remembering what I'm remembering.
Seeing what I'm seeing.
Thinking about Charlie's best dying routine.
Remembering him saving a beach-full of conchs.
Seeing him snuggling with B.B.

> *Want some music?* Mandy Kissinger
> asks Momma.

Sure.

Click.

Through the storm we reach the shore
You gave it all but I want more
And I'm waiting for you
With or without you

With or without you
I can't live
With or without you.

Always wondered who that song was about.

Never dreamed it might be Charlie we were
        living without.
I could live with him, always could.
Wish I could have one more day with him.
I don't know how to live without him.
Don't know that I can,
Don't know that I even want to try.

2

Charlie's ashes ride in Lopez' squad car.
Lights and siren on all the way from Ashland.
Charlie would like that.

The siren goes silent
as they park at the beach.
Another car parks beside
the squad car.
Officer Lopez, Mrs. Lopez,
and Sofia step out of the squad car.
The door to the second car opens.
It's Mr. Nichols.
Officer Lopez carries a shiny container
no bigger than a mayonnaise jar.
They all walk through the sand.
To the fire Curtis
and I built.

Each goes down the line hugging
Momma, Curtis, and me.
Mandy Kissinger joins us.
So does B.B.
He brushes up against legs.
Weaving between one pair,
then another and another.

Like he's looking
for something.
For someone.
We all know who.

Officer Lopez hands the container to Momma.
She squeezes her arms around it.
Kisses it.
Turns.
Walks down the beach
carrying Charlie in her arms.
Her footsteps
a path
in the
sand.

We've brought Charlie back.
Back to the safest perfect place we know.

The waves are gentle.
Barely lapping the shore.
The gulf is turquoise, flat, still.
The orange ball of the sun sits
alone in the blue sky.
I kick at the sand.
Drag my sandal through it.
Form three small trenches.
Side by side.

Down the shoreline
two figures
approach Momma.
Izzy and Gramps.
Momma pulls Izzy
into a hug.
They hold each other.
Gramps pats Izzy's shoulder.
Then Momma's.
Izzy hands Momma
a bunch of flowers.
Gramps and Izzy
walk back up the shore
with Momma and Charlie.

You gonna be writing about all this, Mandy Kissinger?

> *Yes, Calvin*, she answers.
> *Are you okay with that?*

I look down at the
three trenches at my feet.
Yes. I'm okay with that.
Look out on the gulf and the spot
where the sky touches the water.
Everyone needs to know about Charlie.
The world needs to know how hate and fear killed
>   *my brother.*

> *I agree*, Mandy says.

447

*I want you to put something I wrote in the paper.
Can you do that?*

    Probably.

No. Will you do that?

    *Yes, Calvin. I'll work whatever it is into my
article.*

Promise?

    Promise.

I hand her a sheet of
notebook paper
folded in fourths.

Thanks, Mandy.

Izzy flashes a peace sign.

I flash one back.
She, Momma, Gramps,
and Charlie—
cradled in Momma's arms—
join us 'round the fire.

Izzy gives Momma
another hug.
Then steps
toward
me.
I move
to her.
I fall into
her arms
as she falls
into mine.
We instantly
begin to cry
in unison.

Like one
person
in deep,
dark pain.
Can't say a word.
There's not a word to say.
Hold each other.
Cry together.
Together.
Izzy and me.
Together.
Without Charlie.

4

Calvin asked me to say something today.
To honor Charlie. To remember and celebrate his life.

Mr. Nichols stands
beside the crackling
fire. The morning
sun beginning to
warm the beach.
Waves leave traces
of foam on the sand.
Gulls soar above us.

Sofia and Calvin know, Mr. Nichols continues,
that music and poetry inspire me.
And I love it when they inspire my students, too.
Calvin told me at the hospital—
before we knew that Charlie was gone—
that he had completed Thursday's homework
assignment.
He had chosen the theme song for his life.
I was surprised that he was thinking about
school with everything else that was going on,
but that's Calvin. He's always thinking.
Calvin chose a song recorded by the Byrds back in
1965.

A song he found in my record collection.
The song is called "Turn, Turn, Turn."
The lyrics are based on a biblical text.
Calvin said it would be a good idea
to read from the original today.
This is from Ecclesiastes 3.

To every thing there is a season, and a time to
every purpose under heaven.

A time to be born, and a time to die; a time to
plant, and a time to pluck up that which
is planted;

A time to kill, and a time to heal; a time to break
down, and a time to build up;

A time to weep, and a time to laugh; a time to
mourn, and a time to dance;

A time to cast away stones, and a time to
gather stones together; a time to embrace, and
a time to refrain from embracing;

A time to get, and a time to lose; a time to
keep, and a time to cast away;

A time to rend, and a time to sew; a time to
keep silence; and a time to speak;

A time to love, and a time to hate; a time of war, and a time of peace.

I step to the fire.
Mr. Nichols reaches out his hand.
I grab it, and pull him close to me this time.
We hug.

It's my turn to speak.
Charlie Todd Johnston.
Son of Carolyn Johnston.
Brother to Curtis and Calvin Johnston,
and Izabelle Lawrence.
He was the grandson of the late Dutch
and Tiny Amos.
He was a first grader at Ashland Elementary and
lived in Ashland, Florida his entire life—except
when he was at the beach.
He had a cat named B.B.
He had a smile as wide as the sky.
And a heart as big as the gulf.

5

**Momma, Curtis, and I wade out into the waves.
Momma carries Charlie.**

I turn to look at Izzy.
Wave for her to join us.
Seems right that our
beach sister comes too.
She wades out.
Stands with us.

Momma opens the jar.
Stares at the ashes.
The remains of her baby.
The last of Charlie.

> *Charlie, I say . . .*
> *We are proud to be your family.*
> *We are honored to have known you.*
> *You will live forever in our hearts.*
> *We love you now and forever.*

Momma scoops out a
handful of ashes.
Closes her eyes.
Squeezes her hand tight.
Holds it to her chest.
Then to her lips.

Kisses her clenched hand.
Opens her fingers and lets the
ashes fall through, into the air.
The wind carries them up, up, up.
Like a baby bird
        learning
                  to
                          fly.
Then the ashes gently drop
into
the
waves.

I go next.
I hold the jar in
the crook of my
arm with the bandaged hand.
Look inside for the first time.
The ashes are gray.
A sad, somber,
lifeless gray.
I reach in the jar.
Run my fingers
through the powdery ashes.
I can't believe this is Charlie.
I don't want to believe it.
I scoop a handful of ashes.
A handful of my brother.
Pull my hand out.
Look down at
my fist.

I swing back my
arm and throw the ashes
as hard as I can.
A puff of dust.
Then gone.

Curtis takes a turn.
Then Izzy.
We continue until the ashes are gone.
The jar is empty.

Izzy throws the flowers—
the ones she picked for Momma
along the beach Charlie loved—
into the waves.

We turn.
Link our arms.
Step through the waves.
Head back to shore as
Charlie drifts away behind us.

At the shore,
Curtis and I stop.
We have one more thing to do.
We look back toward the horizon.
To the place where Charlie's ashes float.
We thrusts our fists in the air and shout,

BLOOD BROTHERS!

DAY 2—WITHOUT CHARLIE
SUNDAY
AUGUST 30, 1987

1

Early Sunday morning there's a knock on the screen door.

Momma's already up.
Izzy and B.B. are asleep in the recliner.
Curtis and I are on air mattresses
on the living room floor.

Come in, Fred, Momma says.

> *Went to town and picked this up,* he says.
> *Thought you'd want to have it.*

As he walks in, he hands a newspaper to Momma.
Charlie's face smiles up from the front page.
Momma clutches the paper close to her chest,
walks out the screen door.
She sits in the hammock.

Rocks back and forth.
         Back and forth.
                  Back and forth.
I see her through the rustling curtains.
She reads every word.
Touches the paper.
Rocks some more.
Holds the paper gently.
Her fingertips touch
the newspaper
one
last
time.

After a while, she stands.
Lays the paper in the hammock.
Walks down the stairs.
Out to the beach.

Izzy goes out. Brings the paper inside.
It's another AP story by Mandy Kissinger.
A story that the whole town, the whole
state, the whole country, maybe the
whole world is reading right now.
Izzy looks at the newspaper.
Looks at me.
Places the paper in my hands.
Good job, Poet Boy.

Everyone will know about Charlie.
Read his obituary.
Know about the fire.
Learn about the Johnston family.
Read about the funeral at the beach.

Right in the middle of the article,
in a box, is a poem.
My poem.
The poem I wrote.
The poem Mandy Kissinger
promised she would get into the paper.
My poem for Charlie.

He was a boy.
Seven years old.
A little boy with HIV.
A boy who got sick from blood.
He didn't ask for that.
It just happened.

He was a boy.
Seven years old.
A boy who loved school and church and friends.
A boy who had all those things taken away.
He didn't ask for that.
It just happened.

He was a boy.
Seven years old.
Whose home was set on fire.
Who died from breathing in the hate.
He didn't ask for that.
It just happened.

He was a boy.
Seven years old.
A boy who loved the beach.
A boy whose ashes rest there forever.
He didn't ask for that.
It just happened.

He was a boy.
Seven years old.
A boy who should not be forgotten.
A boy that no other boy should be treated like.
I'm asking for that.
It should happen.

By Calvin Johnston

ACKNOWLEDGEMENTS

Sometimes authors talk about a story writing itself and how words flowed onto the page. That was not the case with BLOOD BROTHERS. While I knew it was a story I wanted to tell, putting it on the page was a long, difficult process—a process that took more than five years. A journey that took the support of many friends along the way.

I am grateful to my agent, Rubin Pfeffer, who has always insisted that I tell the stories of my heart and the stories that represent who I am and what I believe. I am grateful to Rubin for continuing to stand behind BLOOD BROTHERS as we tried to find the perfect home for the book, an editor who would be a champion for Calvin and his brothers, and a publisher who would bring this story to readers.

That publisher and that home was Reycraft Books. That editor was Wiley Blevins. I'd heard Wiley speak on two or three occasions before it dawned on me that he might be the person who would see the value in bringing this story to readers. Like me, Wiley had seen discrimination against people with AIDS firsthand. His enthusiasm for this story still takes my breath away. I'm grateful to the entire team at Reycraft for their work on BLOOD BROTHERS and especially want to thank Sunita Apte for her thorough readings and helpful notes.

Many friends from my writing community read this book in various stages and gave valuable input. Thank you to Madeleine Kuderick, Jane Jeffries, JC Kato, and Sue Laneve, the earliest readers, who helped in immeasurable ways. And thanks to others who helped me polish later versions of the manuscript, including Shannon Hitchcock, Augusta Scattergood, Moira Donohue, and Aimee Reid. Lorin Oberweger was a supporter and encourager throughout the project and is the best freelance editor I could have asked for.

Other friends and associates stepped up to share their expertise as the book took shape. Thank you to Dr. Kevin Johnson, MD, MS, at the University of Pennsylvania and the Perelman School of Medicine; Lauri Massey of the AIDS Project of the Ozarks; Norma Fisher Liburd, RN, Burn Unit Specialist; and Linda Coad, Retired Pediatric AIDS Unit RN. My good friend, Linda Shute, also shared her knowledge of and experience with Florida's beaches, plant life, and wildlife.

Thank you to Alsace Walentine, Candice Anderson, and the other fine folks at Tombolo Books in St. Petersburg, Florida, for their continued and enthusiastic support of my books. And to my SCBWI Florida friends—especially Dorian Cirrone, Becky Herzog, Candy Barnhisel, Julie Rand, Candice Wolff, Fred Koehler, and Erica Sirotich—thank you for your friendship, critiques, and encouragement.

As always, I'm grateful to my sister, Pat Sanders, who was instrumental in helping me begin my writing journey. To my Tennessee friends who helped me become the person I am today—Chip Alford, Troy Apple, Paul Nance, Danny Harris, Dee Bynum, Jim Hawk, Carolyn Elam, and the late Margaret King—thank you.

And lastly, thanks to my teaching friends and students who for years encouraged me to keep writing no matter how busy life became. Though I'm not with you all on a daily basis any longer, you still inspire me.

Rob Sanders

BLOOD BROTHERS PLAYLIST

Music plays an essential part in BLOOD BROTHERS.
The songs mentioned in the book are ones worth
listening to today.

- "There Is Power In the Blood," words and music by
  Lewis E. Jones, published in 1899.
- "Sunshine In My Soul," words by Eliza E. Hewitt,
  music by John R. Sweeney, published in 1887.
- "With or Without You," words by Bono and The
  Edge, music by U2, copyright 1986. Originally
  recorded by U2.
- "Walk Like an Egyptian," words and music by Liam
  Sternberg, copyright 1986. Originally recorded by
  The Bangles.
- "The Four Seasons," a set of four violin concertos
  composed by Antonio Vivaldi, published in 1725.
- "We Shall Overcome," inspired by African American
  Gospel Singing, members of the Food and
  Tobacco Workers Union, Charleston, SC, and the
  southern Civil Rights Movement. Musical and lyrical
  adaptation by Zilphia Horton, Frank Hamilton, Guy
  Carawan, and Pete Seeger.
- "A Change Is Gonna Come," words and music by
  Sam Cooke, copyright 1964. Originally recorded by
  Sam Cooke.
- "People Get Ready," words and music by Curtis
  Mayfield, copyright 1964. Originally recorded by The
  Impressions.

- "Strange Fruit," words and music by Lewis Allan, copyright 1939. Best-known recording by Billie Holiday.
- "Lift Every Voice and Sing," words by James Weldon Johnson and music by J. Rosamond Johnson. Known as the "Black national anthem," the song was composed for the anniversary of President Abraham Lincoln's birthday in 1900.
- "Times They Are a-Changin'," words and music by Bob Dylan, copyright 1963. Originally recorded by Bob Dylan.
- "We Shall Not Be Moved" also known as "I Shall Not Be Moved." A song originally sung by enslaved people that continues to be sung as a song of protest. The song dates back to the early 19th century American south.
- "He Was My Brother," words and music by Paul Simon, copyright 1963. Originally recorded by Simon and Garfunkel.
- "Turn, Turn, Turn (To Everything There is a Season)," words from the Book of Ecclesiastes, adaptation and music by Pete Seeger, copyright 1962. Originally recorded by Pete Seeger.

A NOTE FROM THE AUTHOR

BLOOD BROTHERS is a fictional story. But it is rooted in truth. A sad, awful truth. The lives of Ryan White and the Ray brothers—Robert, Ricky, and Randy—inspired this story.

Ryan White was the first kid I ever heard about who had AIDS. In 1984, when he was diagnosed with HIV at the age of 13, most people thought HIV/AIDS was a disease that only gay men and intravenous drug users got. Ryan was neither of those. He was a normal teenager living in Indiana. He contracted HIV through a tainted blood transfusion. He was kicked out of school and his mother had to fight for his right to attend. The Whites were mistreated by people in their community in every imaginable way. Ryan even had customers on his paper route cancel their subscriptions because of their irrational fears of his illness.

I was an adult working in a church in Texas when I heard on the evening news that a family with three HIV-positive boys had been burned out of their house. The Ray brothers, like Ryan White and the fictional Johnston brothers in BLOOD BROTHERS, were hemophiliacs who contracted HIV through blood transfusions. The three Ray brothers lived with their mother, father, and younger sister in Arcadia, Florida. Their sister was not a hemophiliac and did not have HIV.

The Ray brothers were kicked out of school because of their diagnosis. Their mother and father did fight in court to get them back in school. The family was asked not to come back to their church. Mrs. Ray did encourage one of her sons to keep a diary to express his thoughts and feelings. A U.S. District Court Judge did order that the boys be allowed back in school.

Dr. C. Everett Koop, then the Surgeon General of the United States, even visited Arcadia to speak on the boys' behalf. Still, the community did not want them. There were bomb threats and death threats, and on August 28, 1987, when the Ray family was away from home, their house was set on fire. Fortunately, no one was injured.

As I sat in Texas listening to the story of those boys, I realized that I lived in a town like theirs. I worked at a church like theirs. I knew kids who went to a school like theirs. I wondered if our school would kick them out. I wondered if our church would turn the family away. I wondered if people I knew would treat three boys with such hate. I wondered if I might. While I hoped we would be different, I couldn't say for sure that we would be.

More than thirty years after the fire at the Ray's home, I wonder how people would treat a family like theirs today. I wonder if things have changed. I hope they have. But to make things different for people with HIV and AIDS, we have to be educated and aware. We have to intentionally take steps to be different.

I hope BLOOD BROTHERS might start a discussion that could make your generation be the first that we can say, without a doubt, would not tour kids like Ryan White, the Ray brothers, or the Johnstons, and would treat them with respect and be brave enough to stand up for them.

THE FIRST DECADE OF AIDS IN AMERICA

1981

- June—Cases of a rare lung infection and a rare, aggressive cancer are first reported in New York City and Los Angeles.
- By the end of 1981, there are 337 known cases of severe immune deficiency and 130 of those cases have resulted in death. All the cases are among gay men.

1982

- September—The CDC uses the term AIDS (Acquired Immune Deficiency Syndrome) for the first time.
- December—An infant, who received blood transfusions, is diagnosed with AIDS.

1983

- A conference is held to determine guidelines for testing blood for HIV. No decision is reached.
- Cases of AIDS in females who have had sex with men with AIDS are first reported.
- U.S. Congress approves funds for AIDS research and treatment.
- CDC states that HIV cannot be transferred through casual contact.
- The first AIDS discrimination lawsuit is filed.

1984

- The cause of AIDS is discovered, and a blood test is developed to diagnose AIDS.

1985

- First commercial drug test for HIV released.
- Ryan White, an Indiana teenager with AIDS, is refused entry into school.
- September 17—President Ronald Reagan mentions AIDS publicly for the first time.
- At least one HIV case is reported in every region of the world.

1986

- The first panel of the AIDS Memorial Quilt is created.
- The virus causing AIDS is officially named HIV (Human Immunodeficiency Virus).

1987

- Award-winning pianist Liberace dies of AIDS.
- The first antiretroviral drug—AZT—is approved by the U.S. Food and Drug Administration.
- A federal judge orders the Desoto County School Board to admit the Ray brothers—Ricky, Robert, and Randy—to school. The boys are hemophiliacs who have contracted HIV. The town is outraged, and the Ray's home is set on fire.

1988

- December 1—declared World Aids Day.
- Ryan White testifies before the President's Commission on AIDS.
- The Pediatric AIDS Foundation is formed.
- The first national HIV/AIDS educational program is launched.

1989

- Congress creates the National Commission on AIDS.
- 100,000 cases of AIDS are reported in the U.S.

1990

- The CDC reports the transmission of AIDS through a dental procedure.
- April 8—Ryan White dies of AIDS.
- Congress creates the Americans with Disabilities Act. It prohibits discrimination against people with disabilities—including HIV and AIDS.
- Congress creates the Ryan White Comprehensive AIDS Resources Emergency (CARE) Act. It provides 220.5 million dollars to use for community-based care and treatment in its first year.
- AZT is approved for use with pediatric AIDS.

1991

- The Red Ribbon Project is launched.
- November 7—NBA star Magic Johnson announces he's HIV positive.
- By the end of the year, 160,969 cases of AIDS had been reported, resulting in 120,453 deaths.

Source: https://www.aids.gov/hiv-aids-basics/hiv-aids-101/aids-timeline/
Source for the last bullet under 1991: http://www.amfar.org/thirty-years-of-hiv/aids-snapshots-of-an-epidemic/

RYAN WHITE AND THE RAY BROTHERS

The stories of Ryan White and the Ray Brothers were the inspirations for the fictionalized story depicted in BLOOD BROTHERS.

- Ryan White became a national spokesperson for the AIDS crises. He was frequently interviewed, featured on TV, and spoke before the President's Commission on the HIV Epidemic. He died on March 29, 1990, shortly before graduating from high school. Four months after his death, Congress enacted The Ryan White Comprehensive AIDS Resources Emergency (CARE) Act in his honor.
- Ricky Ray, the oldest of the Ray brothers, died on December 13, 1992. He was 15. The Ricky Ray Hemophilia Relief Act of 1998 was named in his honor.
- Robert Ray, the middle brother, died on October 20, 2000. He was 22.
- Randy Ray, the youngest of the brothers, is still living.

HIV AND AIDS IN THE USA TODAY

Today HIV is a treatable disease. While there is no cure for HIV, it can be controlled with medication. The medicine reduces the amount of HIV in the body. Treatment is recommended for everyone with HIV, no matter how long they have had the virus. Medication can keep HIV from becoming AIDS and can help people with AIDS to live long, productive lives.[1]

Despite, available treatments, HIV still continues to spread.

- "Approximately 1.2 million people in the U.S. have HIV. About 13 percent of them don't know it and need testing.
- HIV continues to have a disproportionate impact on certain populations, particularly racial and ethnic minorities and gay and bisexual . . . men.
- In 2019, an estimated 34,800 new HIV infections occurred in the United States.
- New HIV infections declined 8% from 37,800 in 2015 to 34,800 in 2019, after a period of general stability.
- In 2019, 36,801 people received an HIV diagnosis in the U.S. and 6 dependent areas—an overall 9% decrease compared with 2015.
- HIV diagnoses are not evenly distributed across states and regions. The highest rates of new diagnoses continue to occur in the South."[2]

[1] https://www.cdc.gov/hiv/basics/livingwithhiv/treatment.html
[2] https://www.hiv.gov/hiv-basics/overview/data-and-trends/statistics

ABOUT THE AUTHOR

Rob Sanders is a teacher who writes and a writer who teaches. He is known for his funny and fierce fiction and nonfiction picture books and is recognized as one of the pioneers in the arena of LGBTQIA+ literary nonfiction picture books. He taught elementary school for seventeen years, retiring in 2020 to dedicate more time to writing. Rob's nonfiction books continue to break new ground, including the first picture books about the Pride Flag, the Stonewall Uprising, a transgender Civil War soldier, a gay presidential candidate, and the first gay marriage in the United States. His work also continues to introduce readers to heroes of the LGBTQIA+ community—from Harvey Milk to Gilbert Baker, from Cleve Jones to Bayard Rustin to Jeanne Manford, and more. His fiction explores friendship, relationships, standing up for others, and being allies. *Blood Brothers* is his first middle grade novel. Rob also pays it forward. He serves as co-regional advisor for SCBWI Florida and is a frequent speaker, teacher, mentor, coach, and critiquer.

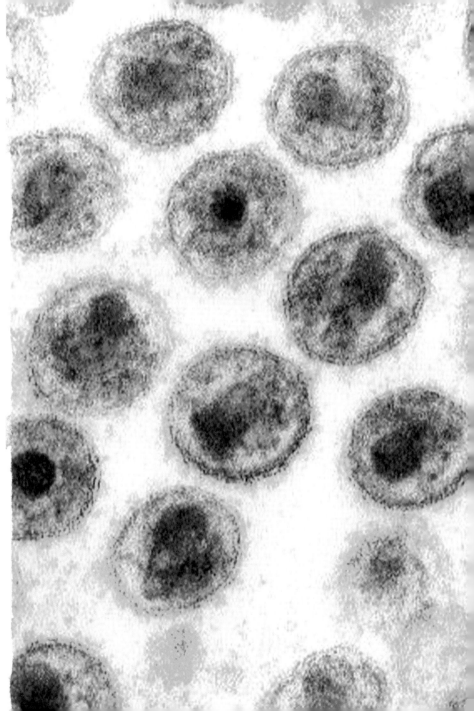

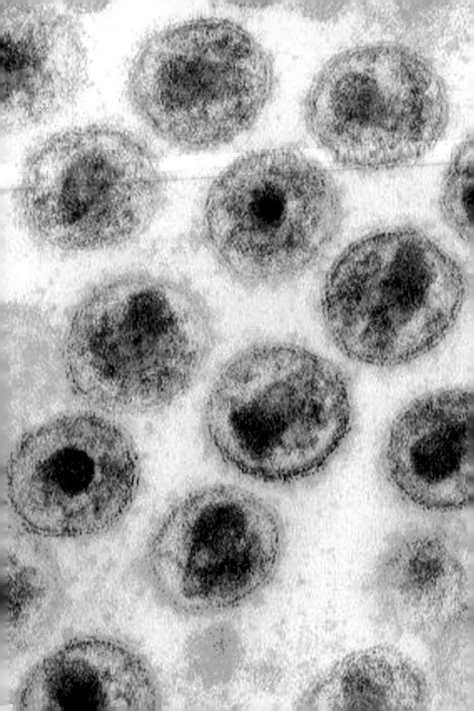